George Burns is an Irish-Canadian author who emigrated from Ireland to Canada in 2010. He currently resides in Vancouver, British Columbia, with his wife, Theresa, and daughter Naoise. Having graduated with an honors bachelor in Civil Engineering, Burns works as a professional engineer and writes in his spare time. When not writing or reading, George can be found hiking and camping all over the lower mainland of British Columbia.

This book is dedicated to my mother. I wish she knew I was writing it. And to my wife, Theresa, who has supported me every step of the way.

George Burns

THE PAGAN'S REVENGE

AUSTIN MACAULEY PUBLISHERS™

LONDON • CAMBRIDGE • NEW YORK • SHARJAH

Ordering Information:
Quantity sales: special discounts are available on quantity purchases by corporations, associations, and others. For details, contact the publisher at the address below.

Publisher's Cataloging-in-Publication data
Burns, George
The Pagan's Revenge

ISBN 9781643788418 (Paperback)
ISBN 9781643788425 (Hardback)
ISBN 9781645365358 (ePub e-book)

Library of Congress Control Number: 2020900842

www.austinmacauley.com/us

First Published (2020)
Austin Macauley Publishers LLC
40 Wall Street, 28th Floor
New York, NY 10005
USA

mail-usa@austinmacauley.com
+1 (646) 5125767

I would like to thank Eamon Kane, for sharing his local knowledge of the battle of Ballaghmoon.

Chapter One

The sky is dark over Western Europe, as the cold harsh weather hammers the shores of its outermost island. She has been shaped by the incessant rain and the wind, having emerged after tens of thousands of years from an ice tomb with her neighboring islands and the rest of mainland Europe.

A vast forested island of green, ringed with ancient mountains, eaten away by the Gods of the Ice Age, broken down by eons of erosion. The black sea crashes on her harsh shores, a lonely outpost on the edge of the Atlantic.

There are no cities to speak of, but countless kingdoms dotted with towns, monasteries, and small settlements.

The Roman Empire is shrinking, having left Britain some four hundred years before. The Vikings are coming from the east to burn the lands of Western Europe and take what they will. In some ways, they will conquer the earth, making their way as far as The New World, whilst ravaging the places they pass through, killing, raping, and taking the spoils of war.

They set their sights all over Europe, eventually becoming the Norman force which will sink her blood-drenched claws into this wild and beautiful Atlantic outpost, never fully letting go. But that is a story for another day.

Seeing the splendor of these harsh lands, the Vikings set sail, fighting the Saxons in Britain, while making their way further west to spill the blood of innocents on an island where there are riches beyond belief. The word of God is ripe. Centers of art and learning are spread throughout this land of saints and scholars. Monasteries are rich in gold and knowledge. A beacon of light and hope for those who would follow. A beacon of greed and opportunity for those who would take.

It is not only from the east that she is attacked. She is torn apart from within like a great sickness inside of her belly, a cancer which will kill her over a thousand years. Her broken factions are constantly at war, where men defile the earth with the blood of those who share a common home, language, and ancestry. Peace is only a dream, something this land has never known in thousands of years. This same dream which will not be realized for another eleven hundred years.

Many wise men walked this land, spreading the word of God and the message of peace. Many wise men ruled this land and hoped and dreamed of peace and unity, but it was not to be. This is the story of one of those men.

Chapter Two

On the twenty-first day of December, in the year of our Lord 883, a storm blew over the Hill of Tara and battered the castle with wind and rain. It lasted for two days and two nights. It is said that the crying of the newborn Princess of Tara, granddaughter to the High King of Ireland, could be heard for miles, over the hiss of rain and the howl of wind, as she came screaming into the world.

She was her father's daughter, a warrior princess. Childbirth was complicated and dangerous in those days, and complications dictated that Gormfhlaith, as she would be named, would have to fight her way into the world, and fight she did, tearing through her mother for freedom to breathe the Irish air, a storm raging in the blackness of early morning in the chamber where she was to be delivered.

She tore her mother, inside the womb that morning, causing her to lose more blood than she could afford. She died shortly after she held the little Princess.

Flan Sinna, Prince of Tara at the time, was just nineteen years old and newly married, having married the woman he loved out of honor as she carried his child. Marriages for the nobles were usually borne out of practicality or the need for an alliance rather than love in those days. A marriage like Flan Sinna and Maobh was rare.

He had argued for four days and four nights with his father, the King, who did not concede until the priest confirmed she was carrying his grandchild. The King, softening in his old age, might have, in his earlier years, have had the woman put to death, but saw how useful it was for his own heir to also have a successor. And besides, a child about the castle would add color to an old man's life.

Flan arrived in the delivery room to see his wife lying in a blood-soaked bed, holding a pink-skinned blob of flesh as the life left her body. She smiled at him through her last breath, trying to whisper the name of her daughter as her soul drifted to the heavens.

The wind howled outside and the rain pelted the wooden walls, it came through the narrow windows, as the child cried, harder and harder, perhaps lamenting over the end of the tragically short relationship with her mother.

Flan, knelt by his dead wife and took her hand, which was already cold, as the nun took his screaming child to clean her.

"A girl," came a voice from behind him. "Hold your daughter, Princess Gormfhlaith."

He didn't realize how long he had been kneeling with his wife's cold, dead hand, but the pink blob had stopped wailing and now resembled a tiny person, wrapped in a brown, woolen blanket.

"Gormfhlaith," he whispered. "That's what she wanted to call you."

"That's what she wanted," replied the nun, handing the child over to the young father.

If Flan Sinna bore any resentment to his daughter, he did not show it. He became King at the age of twenty-three, by which time he had remarried and had two sons, a male heir, more importantly.

His daughter, the little Princess, ran about the castle, always talking, always questioning. She would question the priests about God, about the stars, about the earth, and the sea.

"Who made the stars?" she would ask.

"God made the stars," the priests would reply.

"God made them? Why?" she would always ask, regardless what the subject matter was, she needed answers.

The priests would smile and say, "We do not know, my child, but if you say your prayers every day, he may tell you himself one day."

She would run here and run there, picking flowers, chasing pigs, throwing stones for the hounds, and exploring, until eventually, she found her secret getaway, a tiny hole through the castle walls, just big enough for a small girl to squeeze through and explore the countryside.

From here, she would talk to the surrounding folk, farmers, hunters, and fishers of the rivers, and when her father would get word of this, he would forbid her to go outside the castle walls, but she would still go. In truth, he knew this was no harm, but assigned her a bodyguard anyway. A secret one, who would watch her at a distance.

But the clever little girl always saw the great, big, monstrous soldiers following her like fools from a distance, trying to be inconspicuous, so the King encouraged the friendships she would make so she would always be surrounded by people she knew, whether they be priests or soldiers, bakers or nuns, guards or farmers, the little Princess knew everybody and could never be far from friends.

One such friendship, which blossomed in the summer time of her twelfth year, was with a young soldier, scarcely fifteen years old.

Finnan was the son of a farmer who was indebted to the King. Flan Sinna, being a fair man at the time, forgave the debt, but fairness worked both ways. He expected something in return. This was the lifetime service of the farmer's son, Finnan.

Finnan, a serious boy, was quite taken by the Princess, and was beaten for it when his superiors found out.

When the headstrong young Princess heard of this, she went to her father and screamed and swore, and made threats and ultimatums.

"I will never marry anyone. I am not a Princess," she screamed at him. "You are not my King; you are my father. Is this what fathers do? Beat up their daughter's friends?"

"Gormfhlaith," replied Flan Sinna. "You are a Princess of Tara and you cannot be hanging around with young soldiers."

At this, she screamed at him again, "You are not my King," and ran outside to the kennels, to be with her dogs and to hide her tears.

The King, ever thoughtful in those days, had to think of a solution. He sat up all night, thinking by the candlelight as a storm raged outside, much like that night twelve years ago when the child was born.

The young soldier he resolved would receive the best training. He would be carved into a powerful warrior and he would guard the Princess day and night, and above all else, he would never lay a finger on her, something he did not feel was necessary to mention to the little Princess.

And so the little Princess became a young and beautiful woman with her ever present, somber, bodyguard, always within sight of her, or outside her chamber as she slept.

Chapter Three

It was on a cold December day close to her birthday, when word came to the castle of a wedding.

Gormfhlaith always knew her place in Irish society. The place of a royal or noble daughter was to forge alliances.

She shivered as she walked barefoot on the cold flagstones to visit her father. "You are to be married, my daughter," he said.

"I'm to be married?" she asked, with her hands balled in fists, resting on her hips. "I don't want to get married. Who am I supposed to marry?" she demanded. "When? Why? I won't do it."

Flan Sinna buried his head in his hands and rubbed his face vigorously. The headaches were becoming more frequent these days, and the only thing that could dampen the anger that accompanied them was ale and wine.

He looked back at her in silence; it did not bother him that he was condemning her to a loveless marriage with an old man. An old bishop at that. Alliances were needed and she would do her duty. The Norse threat was ever present. Not to mention the threat from the other Gaelic families and the Saxons across the water. He needed his neighbors feeling secure in themselves, not looking over their shoulder at who might attack them from behind. And besides, it was time his daughter was married. And a royal marriage it would be too.

"But you didn't marry a royal," Gormfhlaith argued, "My mother wasn't a Queen or a Princess."

"I did," he replied. "Not my first wife, yes, but my second."

"You're impossible," she said, and turned to leave, marching to the large wooden door. She came to an abrupt halt when she realized it was barred from the outside, her loyal bodyguard, who obeyed the King's orders first, sealed the door tight shut until he heard otherwise from the King.

"Open it," she screamed, banging on the door. "Open the door. Finnan, open the door. Finnan," she shouted, red in the face. Calling on him for help like she always did. Whenever she wanted to rant or rave about her father or some other incident that irritated her, Finnan would be there, listening, silently nodding and agreeing.

"As you wish, my Queen," he would say. "As you say, my lady."

Finnan did his duty to the last and bolted the door. He had a good idea what the topic of discussion was to require such drastic measures. He stood outside, arms folded across his chest, and listened to the Princess pound on the door and shout his name in anger. He ignored the quizzical looks from the passing servants and guards and tried to look interested in the dull wooden wall across the corridor.

When he was fifteen years old, Flan Sinna had told him that he would be given special training, taught his letters and numbers, religion and language, and trained to be the hardest, toughest warrior that the Hill of Tara had known. This was the same time that it was made known to him that he would be with Gormfhlaith for life. With her, in the sense that he would protect her and be her father's eyes over her.

He would never have any reason to touch her or joke with her, or become overly familiar with her. He would be her personal bodyguard and under pain of death nothing more.

"Gormfhlaith," said Flan Sinna, "do not make me come to you as your King, because I can and I will."

"You are not my King," she shouted at him. "You are not my King. You're not my King. You are my father. What is wrong with you?"

"You're to be a Queen. A Queen, Gormfhlaith," he pleaded, wincing as his head ached; he sat down heavily in a wooden chair.

"A Queen in a land I do not know, to people I do not know, with a husband I do not know," she said, slumping to the ground in frustration, thinking of the farmers and priests and soldiers and guards and all the ordinary folk she had gotten to know about the castle in her youthful wanderings.

"You will have your guards, and your personal servants," Flan replied.

"My guard? Why would you bring Finnan into this? Why would you mention him?" She was about to pound on the door again, when she realized the man she was shouting about was standing on the other side.

"I didn't," the King replied, raising an eyebrow.

Gormfhlaith was almost sobbing now. Almost, for she rarely cried. She was too strong to show weakness. The harder the situation, the more important she thought it not to shed a tear.

"My child, you will marry this man and that is the end of it."

"I will not," she said, sullen defiance in her voice.

They remained inside, Gormfhlaith slumped on the ground, her back against the door, and the King sat in his chair, looking down on her,

15

contemplating what he was sending her to. A childless life, it was likely that Cormac was beyond the years of being capable of producing seed. *Not the priority,* he thought to himself, as he turned away from her and walked to the nearby bed, not for him at least. His sons already provided him with grandchildren. He would have to be honest with her, he thought, as he sat on the sheepskin bed cover.

"He is an older man, and a powerful man at that, for he is the King of Munster. A bishop too. Close to God," he said, as he searched her face for a reaction.

"You met him once when you were small," her eyes flickered over to him.

"You asked him about his horse and he gave you some berries."

"I remember," she said. "He was a kind man. And handsome too, I think."

"You were too young to know what handsome is, but yes, he was and is a kind man. He has the heart of a scholar, not a warrior. Not like me."

"Yes," she said. Her voice was flat like the clang of a weak blade. She had three options. Runaway, die, or marry an old decrepit bishop.

"I will die before I marry him," she said, looking her father straight in the face.

"No, you won't."

"No, I won't, but those are my choices, die or marry."

"Gormfhlaith, don't say that," Flan pleaded again, his headache was growing worse. He walked toward her as she got up.

"Tell him to open the door, you will have your wedding."

It is Flan's wedding, she thought, as she heard the door bolt lift. "You might as well marry him yourself and bugger the old Bishop up the arse," she shouted back over her shoulder as she left. "It amounts to the same thing," and then, despite her mood, she smiled at the image and left her father to stew on her words.

There was no going back, both of them knew, unless the bishop dropped dead. *Then, there would only be another,* she thought. He was a kind man at least, she reminded herself as she walked past Finnan. She kept her head down as she passed him and said nothing else.

"She will get over it," Flan told himself, as he poured himself some ale. She would have servants and guards, ladies and friends, and books and horses, he thought. He proceeded to drink, didn't stop until he was fully immersed in a drunken, foul-smelling stupor, so he could forget his political problems merging with his family life for a while.

****

16

She knew she had to speak to him. She had no duty to him and owed him nothing, Finnan was her bodyguard, but she felt it. She had to make it right with him. *But why?* she thought. "Because I have to," she said to herself. She would not admit the reason to herself, rather pretend it was some vague courtesy. She could not confront the feeling in the back of her mind.

"Finnan, I am to be married," she told him when they were eventually alone together. She had avoided him as best as she could, for days.

"Best wishes, my Queen. I am happy for you," Finnan replied, his voice was low and his face as impassive as a wooden block.

Did it ever change? she thought. *Is the man a stone with no feeling?*

"You are happy for me?" asked the Queen-to-be, her tone sharpened.

"I am," he replied. They stood facing each other in the garden. The birds sang as they spoke and dark clouds rolled in overhead, hinting at the rain that was to come.

"And are you happy for yourself?" she pressed.

"My lady?" he asked, raising an eyebrow. "What has it to do with me?"

"Never mind. Why can't you just talk to me, Finnan? We used to talk."

"What would you have me say?"

"Say what you want," she shouted suddenly, jumping forward. "Say what you feel. Say anything, but not what I expect or what you feel you are supposed to say," she ranted on. She knew she was going too far, saying too much, but she could not help herself. The impassive plank opposite her infuriated her. "Lie to me," she shouted, she was red in the face; a small vein throbbed at her temple. "Shout at me. Sing. Laugh. Do anything," she screamed, "But do something different."

"If you would like to be alone, my lady?" Finnan asked, stepping back.

"Yes. Go," she shouted. Finnan turned to leave but paused. A silence hung between them. The birds even hushed.

"I'm to be a Queen, you know."

"And what of me if I may ask?" his eye twitched. It was small, but she noticed it. They had known each other for an eternity. They had been friends forever. What were they now?

"That's more like it," she retorted. "What of you?"

"I am to remain here?" he asked, his voice was calm.

"You're my personal bodyguard, you are to come with me."

"Your father will not allow that. My place is with him."

"Your place is with me, Finnan," she pointed at him. "When have you ever served my father? It has always been my side you have been at. Your place is with me," she said, jabbing her forefinger into his chest. "You will remain my guard," she let that hang in the air, but Finnan made no reply. "Would that please you?" she asked after a moment.

"As my lady wishes, I am here to serve."

She threw her arms up in the air. "Again, nothing. The statue will say nothing," she shouted. "What is wrong with you?" she went on. "As I wish," she said, "you will do as you are told, like a sniffing dog and follow the bone. Why can't you just speak plain? Is that the extent of the conversation we are to have about this?"

Finnan gritted his teeth. "Yes, it is," he said. "I will be your dog and I will follow the bone. I will stay by your side and watch you marry and grow old with another man." His voice shook, and his face was even redder, "That is what you have asked of me and that is what I will do. Now, if you have no further need of me…"

"I didn't mean it like that, Finnan. Finnan. Why must you be like this?" He was already gone.

****

Four months later, in April, Flan's wedding, as Gormfhlaith liked to call it, took place on a breezy, sunny day, on the Hill of Tara, in the castle of the High King of Ireland.

Guests had come from all over Mide, Leinster, and Munster, some had even crossed the water from the Frankish and Saxon lands.

This was one of the rare days when Finnan was not tethered to his head-strong lady, so he grabbed a goblet of wine and walked the grounds. The bitter wine made him grimace; he had no love for it, but he sipped from the cup regardless. He was too disciplined to get drunk even on a day as dark as this for him.

The man she would marry was older than Gormfhlaith, too old to give her children. He was tall and thin, slender like a tree. Tall, but anchored with strong roots. *This one will not blow over easily*, Finnan thought, as he glimpsed the spark in Cormac's eyes. He was a scholar and a man of peace, Finnan knew, and what he lacked in muscle and ruthlessness, Finnan could see; he made up for it with sharp wit.

Finnan wandered through the gathered guests, listening to and sometimes joining in conversations, moving here and there as the breeze flicked the red and blue flags of Tara above their heads.

****

18

Gormfhlaith was not nervous as she walked slowly to the altar to meet her husband and be wed. She was neither nervous nor excited. Not even happy. "How do you feel?" Deirdre had asked her. "Are you overjoyed? You're about to become a Queen."

Deirdre's fat, red face was almost bursting with excitement. Her grin was so wide, it almost opened her head into two pieces. "Deirdre, I am only delighted," answered Gormfhlaith. "Isn't that obvious?" she asked, her brow creased in a frown.

Poor Deirdre was too dim or intoxicated with excitement to notice, and continued to babble on. "A King," she said, "and a man of God. Your children will be blessed."

"Children?" asked Gormfhlaith, raising an eyebrow. "Are you so silly that you think that man is capable of getting me with child?"

"Oh, my lady," replied Deirdre, shushing the soon-to-be Queen, as she placed a gold ringlet in her hair, "You mustn't say those things."

"Deirdre, the only urges that man gets in the middle of the night is the urge to pray or the urge to piss, nothing more."

"No, my Queen, you will show him different."

"I doubt that," returned Gormfhlaith, rising. "And you forget, I'm not your Queen, and never will be. I'm to be Queen to some damned people I've never known. Where is Finnan? Where is my father?"

Deirdre kept her wide mouth shut this time, as she finally realized she wasn't making matters any better.

****

Cormac stood at the altar of the chapel in Tara and waited.

He wore a purple cloak, emblazoned in red with a wolf's head, the emblem of his family. He was late in his fiftieth year, but he stood tall and solid in his war armor, wearing his crown of silver. He left his bishop's habit behind. Today, he was solely King of Munster. He faced his friend, Meonach, an ancient priest, stooped and slow of speech. He was old and well-traveled, having traveled throughout the Saxon lands to the east. He had been to visit the Franks and Rome to see the Holy Father.

Gormfhlaith could only see his back as she approached from the back of the stone chapel. All eyes were on her, apart from the man she was to marry. He could have been a young man from what she could see.

Cormac, her husband-to-be, remained rigid, as she joined him at the alter in front of the old priest who was starting to drone on in Latin, his bleary eyes fixed on the two who were to be joined.

Cormac was a pious man and took matters of God seriously. His face was somber, but when he turned to her to take her hand, she saw the kindness in his eyes and felt the reassurance of his grip, holding her fingers in such a way, as if to say he would hold her always in safety.

The ceremony of Flan's wedding was long and drab, and the old priest was laborious in the proceedings. The rain pounded the wooden roof of the chapel.

They knelt and prayed, and made vows, and were blessed, and then feasted long into the night until the time came, the next morning, to leave this place she called home under a banner of peace, the dawn of a new age for the two families and the two Kings.

Chapter Four

The night was black, but there was a faint red glow to the sky ahead. Cormac had marched across the sea, walking on the water like Christ himself, in pursuit of the light and now, he climbed through the rain. His feet were bare and bled on the sharp stone steps. The island was sparse and devoid of trees. Little life stayed here, apart from those birds with the colorful beaks who flew from the cliffs. The wind whipped and snapped at his cloak, as he climbed higher and higher, hundreds of steps.

Dark clouds gathered overhead, as he grew conscious of the hour. He felt rushed. Felt that he was running out of time. He had to get to the top before darkness fell. He quickened his steps, planting his tall, dark walking staff hard on the stone as he climbed. He felt he was growing older and older with each step as he climbed.

After many dark, slippery stone steps, he came to the top, as the sun was low on the sky hidden by dark storm clouds across the sea. He turned his gaze east, in search of the mainland, but the height he had climbed made him uneasy and he quit his search. Besides, it was too dark. He turned and stepped through an opening in an old, stone wall and came to a large, stone, beehive hut. In here, he knew there was the one he was looking for. He approached slowly; his bare feet pained him as he stepped into the gloomy hut.

The darkness made him uneasy, but the intense stare of the pale-faced creature within truly chilled him. He was no holy man and though this place may have been a monastery at one point, it was no holy place now. Cormac felt a cold fear creep into his bones, but could not fight the compulsion to walk toward his host and sit on the wooden chair before him. He was transfixed by the man's gaze, it drew him in, dragging him toward the pale, corpse-like messenger.

"I will give you three questions," said the pale-faced man, in a voice like sandpaper.

His face was a mask, showing no emotion. His eyes were steady and fixed. Uncaring and unblinking. His pale skin perfectly smooth. The strangest thing about him was the stillness. His eyes never twitched, his chest never rose or fell, and his gaze never faltered.

He peered at Cormac through a gray-hooded robe and wore a black ring on his index finger. His fingernails were immaculate.

"Three questions," repeated Cormac. He felt he had traveled long and far to put this man to the question and now, here he was. Three questions he could ask, but what were the answers he was seeking? He did not know.

It was told in the ancient stories, that one did not grow old on the island of the youth, so one could have an eternity to consider. Cormac did not believe such superstition, but he did believe that the man who sat before him was privy to knowledge of unimaginable value.

Still, he would not hurry. He deliberately paused to calm his nerve. His fear was reaching delirium and he had to collect himself. His companion's stare made him uneasy. He could see no life or soul or happiness in this man's pale, icy, blue eyes. There was no warmth in his pale skin. No welcoming in his pale hands as they rested on the small wooden table. It seemed as if he would wait on questions for an eternity.

"What is this place?" Cormac asked without thinking.

"This place is a message," came the reply instantly, without hesitation. "It is a warning from across time and distance, to give you a chance to be the savior."

A message, thought Cormac. *How could a place be a message? The savior?*

Silence, as the man waited, unblinking. He closed his eyes, thinking carefully.

"What am I to save?" he could not hide his uncertainty. He never lost his nerve, but this was a strange place and time was strange here. He needed answers.

"They are coming," replied the pale man in the grey robe in an instant. "They are coming from across the sea, in greater numbers than you can imagine, the iron men on the iron horses. They serve the Iron King. They will come to your island and take everything. They will suck you up and feed on you for a thousand years, only to spit you back out a broken and divided mess."

"The Norsemen," he said aloud. "The Norsemen are coming to take everything." They had already started raiding their lands from the river.

The pale-faced man shook his head slowly from side to side, to disagree, but would volunteer no more until Cormac asked his third and final question.

The rain grew heavier outside the hut. He opened eyes to find himself lying on his bed at Thomand. The dream was fading.

****

The alliance between Leinster and Munster had always been unstable. One had continually raided the other, until Cormac had married the High King's daughter, forcing Ceirbeall, King of Leinster, also a friend to Flan, to grudgingly accept a truce. The peace was silent, a standoff more than an agreement, like two angry neighbors eying each other over a stone wall. The presence of Ceallach, blood son to Ceirbeall, and foster son to the King of Munster, did nothing to stop his blood father's raids in the past. To some, it seemed as if Ceirbeall did not care if his son was killed in retribution. Being a pious and peace-loving man, Cormac had agreed to stop the retaliation against Leinster's borders.

They say it takes a great celebration to bring people together, and that is what happened. The enemy of my enemy is my friend, a wise man once said. The friend of my friend is what? A friend, one supposes? This is what Cormac supposed when he proposed to Flan Sinna that he marry his daughter, Gormfhlaith, bonding the two kingdoms through marriage, and therefore, bonding Leinster and Munster through mutual alliances.

And as a love and respect grew between Cormac and his beautiful, new bride, trade developed between Munster and Leinster, every full moon, goods would be exchanged and drinks shared. Though it kept the bloodshed at bay, the friendship did not grow. Ceirbeall, the King of Leinster, had betrayed many friends in the past for the betterment of his position, and rumors from Mide said that Flan Sinna, too, was becoming more and more unpredictable in his behavior.

"We must appease our neighbors," Cormac had told Flaithbertach, as they sat opposite each other, stooped over a chessboard, the candlelight cast the shadows of the pieces off the stone walls, like strange demons dancing about the room.

"Appease them, my King?" Flaithbertach asked.

Flaithbertach was a tall man, with a great, thick, black beard, and a scar running down the left side of his face, scarcely a finger's width from his eye. He wore the clothes of an abbot, but had the build of a warrior, for he was both of those things. He was the Abbot of Innis Caithigh, an island to the west, many hours from the coast. His opinion and wisdom were valued in Cashel.

"Yes, Flaithbertach. Through trade. I fear them."

"Fear is a weakness we cannot afford, my King." The two men had been friends since Cormac had washed ashore, shipwrecked, and half dead on Innis Caithigh, the island of Flaithbertach's monastery, many years before.

Flaithbertach, though he was a man of God, had left behind a life of violence and he still carried the anger and suspicion of his previous life with him, something Cormac continually tried to ease from his friend's mind.

"No, Flaithbertach, you are wrong," Cormac said, moving one of the carved stone pieces. "Fear is simply the mind cautioning the self. A brave man is one who feels fear, yet confronts it," Cormac went on. "Only the fool is not afraid. We are not fools, Flaithbertach," he said.

Flaithbertach would leave his island for Thomand, to visit Cormac, every second moon, and remain for a week or sometimes more, providing council and news. He would sometimes travel elsewhere also, always alone. Everywhere he went, he was armed and could kill any man with the swing of his short sword, which he had christened 'the darkness,' another remnant of that previous life he tried, but failed to leave behind. He could never do that, and deep down, he knew that. Sometimes, he craved the violence. Sometimes, he craved the blood. That is when he would pray, but often, he felt like his prayers were not heard.

"No, indeed we are not fools," Flaithbertach replied, looking up, his face shrouded in gloom. "You fear Leinster, my King?"

"I fear them all, Flaithbertach. The Leinstermen, the Connaughtmen, the Norsemen. We cannot remain divided. I have been having dreams."

Flaithbertach moved his Queen into a forward position. "Dreams?" he asked, as he clenched his teeth together, "What have dreams got to do with anything, my King? Dreams are dreams."

"Never mind, another time." Cormac stood, "I'm sending you to Leinster. I want you to get the measure of King Ceirbeall, judge what you can of his intentions. You will go under the pretense of trade and take gifts of grain and mead in exchange for whatever they want to offer." He sighed, "The last thing I want is war with this man, but if it is coming, I want to know about it."

"Why don't you ask Ceallach?"

"Ceallach is a boy, Flaithbertach, you are wise and learned beyond your years and you are no longer a young man. This is not a job for boys, especially pitting a son against his father. Maybe in time, I will send him, but not now."

They remained silent. The game was left unfinished, the stone pieces standing on the board, like silent soldiers waiting for their orders. The candle burned down and they finished their wine and sat in silence. Neither felt the urge to break it, Cormac prayed silently to his God to ease his worries, Flaithbertach wondered where his God was and if he even listened.

****

"I can make you a King."

"Come again?" Flaithbertach asked. He sat with Ceirbeall, the King of Leinster. He had arrived in the morning after traveling four days and four nights, having left Thomand the morning after his conversation with Cormac. He was not one to waste time.

"I said, I can make you a King, Flaithbertach," Ceirbeall's voice crackled like a reptile. The two men eyed each other in the torchlight, over a long wooden table laid out with food.

Ceirbeall was a clever one, Flaithbertach knew. Dangerous, waiting to strike.

"Speak plainly, man. What are you talking about?" Flaithbertach returned. He cast his eyes to the floor as his heart quickened. This was a dangerous place.

"I have heard stories about you…priest," he let the last word slide out slowly, as if it was a piece of grizzle from the steaming pork in front of them.

"Priest?" Flaithbertach repeated. He looked up as he mulled the word over in his mind. He swallowed his meat and took a gulp of wine. "Yes, so what?" he asked.

"A priest who worships the old Gods," Ceirbeall went on.

"What do you care, Ceirbeall?" he put down his cup and sat back, watching the King. "Are you such a God-fearing Christian all of a sudden that you give a shit about my religious inclination?"

Ceirbeall smiled again across the table and lifted his heavy, muscular arms in mock apology.

The light had faded outside now, the sun was down. Flaithbertach would be spending the night, he would have been, one way or the other, he thought, but he preferred the open country to a den of snakes. The silence dragged on. *Dangerous words had been spoken,* Flaithbertach thought.

"Does it interest you, brother?" Ceirbeall asked again.

"Dangerous words," he said. "Does what interest me? Stop your games and speak plain, man. I am here to discuss the friendship between Leinster and Munster, and its continuation, so speak, man, and let your thoughts be known."

"Do not forget yourself, Flaithbertach," Ceirbeall's tone changed. The sneer was gone now, "I am a King and you are in my halls." His eyes matched Flaithbertach's stare, "Very well, I will speak plainly then. I will speak plainly and I expect to be answered plainly." He paused. A dog barked outside and the logs cracked in the fire. "Does it interest you?" he asked again.

"Does what interest me, Ceirbeall?"

Ceirbeall slammed his giant fist into the table with such force that it sent meat and grease flying into the air, and upended the jugs of wine, the red liquid dripped off the side of the table and prompted two slave girls to scurry over.

"Leave it," Ceirbeall roared at them and got to his feet. "Get out of my sight or I'll cut your hands off. Out!" he roared.

25

Flaithbertach was surprised at the reaction, but he was not afraid. Ceirbeall was a man, and men can only cause physical pain. Flaithbertach did not fear physical pain.

"It does," he found himself say, to his surprise. Did it interest him? He did not know. How could it? He was one of the closest advisors to the King. "But not so long as it is occupied," he added. "Let that be an end to this line of discussion," he said.

Ceirbeall stood facing Flaithbertach, his shaved head shining with a film of sweat, but his face was a mask of calm, "You answer plainly, that is all I can ask. Our friendship with Munster will continue." He picked up the fallen jugs, "I will arrange a gesture to prove, as much by the next full moon. We are finished here, priest. Think on what I said, and if it is spoken of to the wrong people, I imagine that would lead to a fight where there would be no winners. Sleep well." With that, he left and said, "I will send those two slave girls to lie with you tonight"

"Keep them for yourself," Flaithbertach replied.

****

The measure of the man.

Flaithbertach had indeed gotten the measure of the man. Ceirbeall had told him all he needed to know in one night, and he was saddled and ready to go the next morning before dawn. This was a dangerous place and he felt he should stay no longer. He had four days hard riding back to Thomand, and though he did not really believe it, there was a chance that Ceirbeall would regret his loose tongue the night before and send someone in pursuit to rectify that. The sly King's serpent words lingered in Flaithbertach's mind, tempting him, like the devil with Christ in the desert. Life was temptation and the devil had snares everywhere. But was it the work of the devil? he wondered. "I can make you a King." *A King,* he thought. At one time, that is what he had wanted. That is what he had fought for. To be the leader of men. But that dream was long gone. He would deliver his message to Cormac and let him know what had transpired, and tell him that Ceirbeall was not to be trusted. His motives were neither divine nor just. He would then return home for silent prayer and fasting, to flush the sinful cravings from his mind.

The old Gods, Ceirbeall had also mentioned the old Gods. He thought of the old Gods he had worshiped, before his parents were taken from him in a rush of hate and anger. His skin tightened. His head felt warm as he rode. He fixed his mind to the crucifix, and Jesus, dying on the cross to save his people from their sins, and he felt…nothing…he thought of Jesus and he felt nothing.

He spat to one side and rode harder to deliver his message and be rid of this place as soon as possible.

****

The Norse attacks had grown more frequent and it bothered Flaithbertach. It was only a matter of time before his island was attacked. Innis Caithigh lay in desolation, a vulnerable and isolated island, about a mile off an empty shore. They were not a rich monastery, they had some gold on the island, but not much. Despite this, it was still a target for the Norsemen.

Flaithbertach considered this, as he sat in silent contemplation in the chapel. He had asked Cormac, his friend and King, on more than one occasion, to act on the Viking problem. He had encouraged Cormac to open talks with their neighbors, with a view to an attack on Dublin and maybe, in time, on to the Isle of Man or York. He was continually frustrated to find his pleas were falling on deaf ears. Why did he refuse to strike at the Norse devils?

They were coming. It was only a matter of time. Cormac was relatively safe, nestled closely inland, but out here, on the coast, exposed, this was a different story.

It was midmorning now, and the sun shone in through the narrow window on the east side of the small stone chapel. It had stopped raining now, and the wind had died down somewhat. The seas would soon be calm enough to make a crossing.

He watched the candle flicker on the simple, undecorated, stone altar, as he thought about his conversation with Ceirbeall. Flaithbertach was a logical man and the suggestion made sense, but taking power in Munster was something that he could not do. There were so many reasons, among them, the fact that the King of Munster was his friend. It could not be achieved without bloodshed, and Flaithbertach had left that life behind him. He knew he would make a great King. A better King than Cormac, but this was not for discussion. He had ended the matter with Ceirbeall and left Leinster, planning to report everything back to Cormac. Something had stopped him, though. He did not tell Cormac about his discussion with Ceirbeall. Why was he holding onto it, like a chess piece waiting to be played? He would make a better King than Cormac, and he would address the Viking problem.

"NO!" he said to himself aloud, standing suddenly, surprising himself by the sound of his voice in the cavernous silence of the chapel. Another brother, deep in prayer, glanced over at the interruption. Flaithbertach ignored him, quickly genuflected, and turned from the altar to leave.

This would continue to eat away at him until he told Cormac about Ceirbeall and their conversation. He should prepare a boat and make for Thomand once the seas permitted.

It was two more days before the wind died down, enough to permit a crossing to the mainland. Flaithbertach had loaded the small leather curragh and taken two brothers with him. They would be given horses on the shore for the two-day ride to Munster.

It was there, in the sand beach of the mainland, as Flaithbertach and his two brothers secured the curragh and prepared the horses for the ride, that his keen eyes spotted the red and white striped sails of a Viking longboat making its way swiftly along the horizon. Flaithbertach squinted against the glaring sun, but knew there was no mistake. He knew what he saw. He couldn't make out the details, but the sail was enough to put the feeling of dread back into his stomach.

"Back to the boat," he shouted. "We don't need the horses, we're heading back to the monastery."

The crossing had taken five hours as the sea was still rough. By that time, the Vikings had arrived at Innis Caithigh and taken what plunder they could find.

Flaithbertach dragged the boat ashore with the help of his two brothers. He dropped his sword, the darkness, in the sand. He knew the Vikings had already left as he ran, his breath heaving, for the burning chapel. The smell of death hung in the air, he stopped and dropped to one knee as he vomited in the dew-damp ground underfoot.

He watched the black plumes of smoke rising slowly, lazily from the blackened shell of the building. It resembled a great, rotting, whale carcass. He watched as he imagined the souls of his brothers floating up with the smoke.

Upward to where? he thought bitterly. *What God would allow this to happen?* Images of the old Gods flashed through his mind as he knelt before the burning church, he could see the ancient Celtic symbols swirling through the smoke as he watched it billow upward to the sky.

He fell back to the ground and lay on his back.

The rain began to fall on his upturned face, mixing with tears of rage, as he asked himself, *What God would allow this to happen? Not the ancient Gods of this land*, he thought. The Celtic Gods could defeat the Norse Gods, as Christ stood idly by, nursing his wounds, as he watched his servants burn.

"What King would let this happen?" Flaithbertach screamed aloud, as the heavens opened and the rain beat down on his face.

"Not I," he shouted, as he thumped his chest and sat up. "Not I," he screamed. The rain came down in heavy sheets now, drenching the screaming monk, as the sky blackened overhead. Thunder rumbled in the distance as Flaithbertach screamed, his voiced merged with the rumble from the heavens and he became one with the storm in his rage.

****

The rain that so often batters the lonely Atlantic coast came down with such force that night, that it quenched the fires of the burning church, as if God himself was sending the flood a second time, to purge the earth of evil.

The wind howled through the desolated stone huts, taunting the three remaining monks who huddled in the blackness of night, the darkness shading their grief like a blanket.

Flaithbertach slept fitfully, his dreams were haunted by the wisps of smoke rising from the church. The souls. *Where were they going?* he thought. The smoke was rising. As the flames were dying away, he gazed at them and saw flashes of the spiral images his pagan parents had worshiped. They flashed through his mind, the dying flames seemed to take their shape, twisting and swirling, as if the sky was a stone in which these ancient symbols were etched.

As dawn approached, the storm died away in time with the flames, as if its only purpose was to quench the burning church. The red glow of the flame was replaced by a golden hue in the west, as the sun rose over the wild, gray ocean.

The burning embers hissed as Flaithbertach approached the collapsed door of the chapel. He kicked it open and stumbled in to a scene of blackness. It was as if a drunken party had been turned to charcoal by some mischievous spirit. The ceiling had collapsed, covering many of the dead monks. He could see where they had crowded at the door, trying to smash through it with a wooden pew, but to no avail. They fell and perished, leaving only the charcoal-black skulls grinning back at Flaithbertach, as if some trick were played on him. And maybe the joke was on him. He had left to plead with Cormac again. He should have been with his brothers. At least with his fighting experience, he could have done something.

He stepped over the charred remains, the smell of cooked flesh stung his nostrils and the smoke made his eyes water. He walked up the aisle to the altar, which he had built himself, and there, still kneeling, facing God, was the burned body of a monk who had not tried to flee, Edmund. It had to be Edmund. This one had not tried to break down the door and run to the axes of the waiting Viking devils or tried to climb through a window far too small for him. This one had remained in prayer, crouched before God, and had burned to death in prayer.

29

Flaithbertach dropped to his knees beside the blackened bag of bones and fell forward before the alter, and wept in the ashes, the spiral pagan images hammered through his mind as he struggled to communicate with a God that would not listen.

His chest tightened and his head pounded like a drum. The grinning skull beside him screamed at him. He could see the fire engulfing it. He could hear the screams of the monks all around him. He got to his feet and fell to one side. The spirals flashed before his eyes again, he could see them burned into the wall behind the altar where the crucifix was. The smoke. He could not see with the smoke, yet the spirals burned through it. The images of the Gods his parents had worshiped, burned in his mind when he closed his eyes tight.

He opened them to silence. He knew where he had to go.

Chapter Five

Finnan settled well in Munster, continuing with his duties to Gormfhlaith, while also taking a prominent part in the King's army. He had found Cormac to be a fair and clever man, slow to anger, and hesitant to draw the swords of his soldiers unless absolutely necessary.

One of his first outings was a cattle raid in the night, where twenty of the King's beasts had been taken. Cattle raids were commonplace as livestock not only kept men alive with milk and meat, but it was a measure of wealth, just as much as gold or silver. Finnan and five of his new comrades had saddled up and tracked the beasts into the nearby mountains, to find twelve men squatting by a fire in the rain, surrounded by the King's animals. They were hungry mountain men, poorly armed and weak, and they surrendered without much argument.

The Munstermen had argued to put these men to the sword, but Finnan had disagreed.

"Our King is a man of God," he had said.

Our King. It was strange to think of this bishop as his King now, but he was getting used to it.

"A man of God, yes," they replied. "Then all the more reason to kill these men. They have stolen from both, a King and a bishop."

"We'll not kill them," said Finnan.

"Says who?" asked Matudan, an ancient one-eyed warrior who only seemed to grow stronger and heartier with age, he was one of Cormac's war chiefs. Though Finnan was not a war chief, he was the personal bodyguard to the King and Queen, and carried as much sway as any chief. "A blow in from Leinster," Matudan said. "To hell with you," he said, as he drew his blade and knocked one of the prisoners to the ground with the hilt of his sword. The man fell heavily in the rain and shivered on the ground like a frightened animal. "We'll finish these bastards."

"Matudan," said Finnan. Matudan was quick to anger always, "You will not. These are not evil men. Simply hungry."

"Hah," Matudan laughed, and raised his sword to the sky, the blade glinted in the sun, as it fought its way through the rain clouds. Before he could bring the blade down, Finnan pounced on him and knocked the sword from his arms, it fell in the mud with a dull thud. "What is this?" Matudan roared, and turned on Finnan.

Finnan did not move. He stared at Matudan, but kept his hands by his sides, he did not draw his weapon. "You will kill them only with the permission of the King," Finnan said.

Matudan spat, "Then we won't be killing them, I suppose." He bent to pick up his sword. "Clean it," he said, and he dropped it at the feet of the man who cowered under him.

The group returned with both cattle and prisoners and not a word of the altercation was mentioned to the King. Cormac, being a fair man, put the men to work for six months and then released them back to the mountains. He promised to sell them any cattle at a more than fair price, and from time to time, sent carts of bread and ale, and offered the men work in the summer on the crops where they could take a small portion. "If only they had come to me before they stole my cattle," the King lamented.

Finnan respected the King for this and saw great virtues in the man, more so than he saw in Cormac's father-in-law, Flan Sinna. Flan was a ruthless man when he wanted to be and grew more ruthless by the day from what he heard. He was glad to be rid of that place. Cormac's power was in restraint and patience. Some would say that was a weakness. Finnan heard whisperings here and there, around the halls of Thomand, about those who thought their King nothing more than a weak, glorified bishop. Finnan always listened for such talk, for his duties were to protect his Queen and in doing so, protect her husband. He would die for both of them if circumstance called for it.

It was for this very reason that Finnan found himself regularly drinking with the ordinary footmen and guards about the castle. Finnan was the personal guard to the King and Queen, and these men had to obey him, though he was not their direct superior. That was Matudan. The bald, old fighter he had started off badly with, in the hills that rainy day with the cattle thieves.

One such night, Finnan found himself sitting with his bottle of ale in the soldiers' common room. A storm raged outside. High winds had come in from the sea, and the rain battered the kingdom of Thomand for the third time in the space of a week. It was night time, and a fire burned. Finnan paced himself as always. He never allowed himself to get drunk, but would hold his drink for many hours before taking a second. The men would drink and joke and talk and dance, and sneak whores in and fuck them, and sometimes, fights would break out, and Finnan would call order as it was expected of him, and he was respected.

He sat, thinking and listening in the corner, as the fire burned and the other soldiers huddled around. There was only seven of them this night, as none ventured too far. This weather weighed heavily on them and the mood was low and somber.

"The mad monk has returned," one of the soldiers said.

Finnan had not heard of the mad monk before, but kept silent. Usually, the answers would present themselves without his needing to ask.

"He's back from his island?" asked another man. "What's his problem now?"

"Well, you know what happened, don't you?" came the reply.

"The Norsemen raided his monastery. He's angry. They burned it to the ground. Nothing even worth robbing in the place. I suppose the bastards were angry at finding it empty and set flame to the chapel."

"With his brothers inside," finished off another old man sitting to Finnan's left, the firelight showed the man's face to be partially obscured by an eye patch. Congall; an old man. He loved the stories and loved to embellish.

"I suppose so. They're dead anyway, far as I hear," answered the man who had been telling the story. Another older man named Seachnaill, who was not from Munster originally, and spoke with a strange accent Finnan could not place. He made it his business to know as much as he possibly could, about every man and woman who could ever be close to the Queen or King.

"The Norsemen are a harsh bunch," Finnan put in. He didn't want to ask any questions, but always had a comment here and there. Enough to be part of the group, but not to give anything away. He didn't want to appear cagey either. He genuinely wanted these men's trust, but also needed their information and insights. He wanted to know how these men thought and needed to know if he could trust them and if they would also die for King and Queen.

"Harsh men indeed. Great men to fight. I wouldn't mind testing myself against them some time," said Congall.

"You're too old," shouted one of the younger men, "They'd cut you down like a twig."

There was an uproar of laughter which was rudely interrupted by a gust of wind through the door, as another soldier came in, his wool cloak was sopping wet from the incessant rain.

"Shut that bloody door," shouted Finnan, as the man dawdled, taking off his wet cloak, while he let the harsh wind drive the freezing rain in. Finnan then got up and slammed the door shut himself.

"Are you trying to kill us or what?"

The man didn't reply, seeing it was Finnan who was berating him, and sat in silence by the fire

"And that's my bastard seat," Finnan shouted.

In truth, he wasn't angry, but these men enjoyed seeing arguments and respected men who were quick to anger. He never fully understood why men responded so well to anger. Especially in a kingdom where their King was trying to forge peace from the harsh countryside.

The men laughed as the newcomer fumbled his words and tripped in his haste to move. The conversation continued for a while to this and that. Vikings and farming. Arm wrestling was mentioned and a challenge was put forward, but nobody was in the mood for it. It was only when the conversation died down and there was a lull, that Finnan reignited the talk of the Vikings and the monk.

"Why do they call him the mad monk?" he asked.

"Because he's mad," came an answer, followed by silence, as the man who gave it stared at Finnan as if he himself were mad.

This was interrupted by more ale-driven laughter.

"No," said the man, throwing more logs on the fire and stoking it, "On a serious note, I suppose you wouldn't have heard of him, Finnan, given that you're here less than a year."

"He's a mad bastard," said another younger man. "That's why."

"We've established that. Now shut the fuck up and don't interrupt me again," said old Congall. You could tell the old warrior, drunk as he was, was settling himself to tell one of his stories.

"Oh for fuck's sake," said Seachnaill, in his strange musical accent. "This will be a long one, Finnan. You'll need this more than me if you're going to sit through it." He handed Finnan the remainder of his ale and left without another word. Congall edged closer to Finnan, staring at him through his one good eye, as the other men either got up to leave or started their own conversations.

"The mad monk, Flaithbertach is his name, you see." Finnan listened with interest. This was the sort of stuff he came for every night, he thought, as the old man spoke. "He is the son of Imnain and the abbot of the monastery on Innis Caithigh. A windswept hole of a place, that you'd have to be mad to live on anyway," continued the old man. "But that's not why we call him the mad monk." He paused to take a gulp of his ale, as did Finnan, the firelight reflected on their faces as the wind howled outside.

"He was a soldier, you see. For many years. I think, he had been a monk in the beginning," Congall screwed up his face in thought, the scar under his eye patch visible for a second as the skin bunched up around it. "That's right, he was a monk in the beginning when he was a young lad, or at least, in training for such. He had a knack for the languages as well. Latin, Saxon, and whatever else they speak over in them lands. He knew the Gods too. The old Gods," he said, pausing for emphasis as he looked Finnan in the eye. "The old Gods indeed," he said again, though Finnan had not reacted. Congall had a habit of seeing a nod or a disagreement in the conversation where there was none. "And the Norse Gods. He knew them too, somehow. His family were of the old Gods. Somewhere on the coast up north a bit. Or west somewhere. West, that was it," he said, nodding to himself.

Finnan continued to listen in silence as the other men lost interest in their own conversation and left one by one, until it was only the two men.

"Me feckin' ale is gone," said Congall, interrupting himself. "Hold on till I get me drink," he said, rising. He was a warrior but Finnan couldn't see much use for him in this light, apart from telling stories.

"Anyway," he said, sitting back down, drink refilled with the bottom of the barrel, "anyway, where were we?"

"Flaithbertach and the Gods," Finnan filled in. The first words he had spoken since the old man had started talking.

"That's right. The Gods," Congall continued, remembering. "Anyways, he grew up with the old Gods, worshiping the stones and all like them fellas do. You know how they are."

Finnan nodded, though he did not know how they are, he lived on a Christian island, as it had been for centuries.

"Yes," said Congall. "And then, he was taken as a slave for the Norsemen, which is why he takes such a dislike to them yellah-headed bastards. But he made some friends among them fuckers too, so he did. He learned to talk their talk and to fight and some way or another, he went from being a slave to a warrior and battered fellas into the ground till they were mush, so he did." The ale ran down his chin as he spoke faster.

"But somehow, he found Jesus at one stage and took a great liking to Jesus, so much so that he rose to be well-respected in the monastery, and eventually, he was the abbot."

"I see," said Finnan thoughtfully.

"Yes. The abbot. Anyway, I think he may have done two stints in the monastery, one before the time with the Norsemen, and one after. But why is he mad, you say?"

"Why is he mad?" Finnan repeated and smiled at Congall. *Warrior or not,* he thought, *I like this storyteller.*

"They say there's nothing he wouldn't do. They say he still worships the old Gods and that he's not a Christian at all. They say he'll stop at nothing to see the Vikings ruined and that is the only reason he councils Mac Cuileneann."

"The King," Finnan corrected.

"Yes, the King," said Congall in agreement, not realizing his slip.

"Don't forget yourself, Congall," Finnan reminded him again, "He's your King. Do not get too familiar."

"Oh yes," he said. "My pardon."

"Anyway, the man is more ruthless than any King. They say when he was a warrior, that he fought side by side with the Vikings and killed babies. They say he killed a thousand men before he found the cross. And some say the cross is only an act. That he's not a Christian at all. He eats men's eyeballs too, apparently," he said, tapping his finger on his own empty socket.

"That's what happened to you then?" Finnan asked. "The mad monk ate your eyeball?"

Congall's one eye narrowed and he leaned over and whispered, "He worships the old Gods. The stones and them devils and fairies and all." His breath reeked of ale.

Finnan did not know what was true and what was false, but he would figure that out for himself. He had a story now. *And stories grew from somewhere,* he thought.

"Goodnight, old man. Come on. We're the last ones here."

They quenched the dying fire and went out into the rain. "The mad monk," Finnan whispered to himself. It would not be long before he met this man, he thought, as he headed for his bed.

****

Cormac retired to his room. His wife was already sleeping. He sat and watched her chest rise and fall in the dim light from a small candle burning by the bed.

There was a pitcher of wine sitting on the table beside him. He poured and drank deep. He had been troubled of late. He pulled his cloak tight around him to keep the chill away. Although it was summer, there was no warmth in the nights, and it rained often.

He turned to his writing desk and took to finishing the parchment he had been working on the day previous. He intended to illuminate the land with a work on the Gaelic language to help those in Rome or England understand their words.

It was not long though, before fatigue caught up on him and he was snoring in the chair, the candle burned down and the room fell dark.

Cormac rarely dreamed, or at least, never remembered his dreams. But of late, the pale-faced man with the unmoving features had visited him. Tonight was another such night.

They sat in his dining hall, sharing a great feast together with a fireplace full of burning logs. "Our friends are the most important thing, Cormac," said the pale-faced man. "Old friends and new friends alike. But more important still, is the ability to be able to tell the difference between our friends and our enemies."

"Very important," Cormac agreed. "Very important indeed. And which are you? My friend or my enemy? We sit here breaking bread as if we are great together, but are you my friend? Should I take your advice?"

"That is exactly what I am telling you, Cormac," the pale-faced man continued. He prodded Cormac in the chest with a long, white forefinger, "You have to decide. You have to decide on me and all these around you."

Cormac looked around the table and saw many people. Faces both familiar and unfamiliar. There was a huge, bearded Norseman on his left, with his hand extended in friendship. Flaithbertach and Finnan were there, both looking dour and sullen. His wife was there. Her hands were tied, placed in front of her on the table. She had no mouth, though her eyes were calm.

As they continued to eat, the Norseman asked, "Will you not take my hand, Cormac?"

"It is for you to decide," said the pale-faced man again. "You must decide."

He looked across the table to Flaithbertach, his great friend and advisor, for an opinion, but could only see a shadowy figure in the dark. Finnan shook his head at him slowly, his piercing, blue eyes giving away little. His wife, Gormfhlaith, was gone now.

Flaithbertach has taken her away, she is tired, he thought.

He then noticed that the dark figure was sitting atop a horse.

"Who is that?" asked Cormac.

"Take my hand," insisted the Norseman again, smiling. "Take my hand and we will see together."

"Who is that?" asked Cormac again of the shadow, he stood to get a better look.

"I told you to take my hand" he heard the Norseman's voice again, more urgent this time, but he was gone.

"You must decide who is your friend," came the pale-faced man's voice. "You must decide," but he was also gone when Cormac turned to face him.

The horseman urged his mount forward into the light, sitting up straight in the high-walled chamber.

I must decide, thought Cormac, knowing full well that this shadowy rider was no friend.

The firelight revealed a huge man, dressed head to foot in the finest steel armor Cormac had ever seen. Such a suit must have been worth a fortune in silver. Even a King could not dress like this. Even his great horse was armored. He looked on Cormac with burning eyes of fire and raised a huge sword, almost the length of his body, in both arms, high above his head, and slammed it down to cut the table in two in one blow.

"You are not my friend," Cormac shouted in horror, as the ashes in the fireplace was scattered and the room started to burn. Cormac felt his spirit soaring out of the room, up in the air over a ravaged, burning landscape, with thousands of these huge horsemen everywhere, cutting, burning, raping, and destroying. He looked to the east to see ship after ship after ship landing on the coast, with more and more of these huge mounted soldiers pouring out.

Then, the earth below him shook and a great chasm opened, tearing the land in half and Cormac fell. Down and down, to be swallowed by the gaping hole which tore the land in two.

He awoke in the darkness, unsure of where he was, until his eyes adjusted and he came to his senses. The uneasy feeling, as if he was falling, still held him. "There is more to this than just a simple dream," he whispered to himself. He would go and wake Meonach. He needed to find some meaning in this.

****

It was late morning on a fine day. The sky was blue and cloudless, a rarity these days. Cormac sat in his private quarters on a high-backed wooden chair, bent over a manuscript, quill in hand, working meticulously on his lettering, like a master craftsman, when a knock came to the door.

He ignored it and continued to write, he was not to be disturbed when he was at his books. It sounded again. "My King," came a voice from the hall outside.

"Yes. What is it?" asked Cormac. "I'm at my books. Come in if you must." The door opened to reveal the blond head of Ceallach, his foster son, poking through the door.

Ceallach was twenty-two years old. Technically, he was a hostage from his blood father, Ceirbeall, the King of Leinster, to ensure peace between the two kingdoms, but he spoke to Cormac in the familiar voice of a son.

"I'm sorry, Father. The soldiers have returned."

"They're back," Cormac acknowledged, putting down his quill and blowing on the wet ink on the page. "What news, then?"

"Prisoners, Father. You should come."

"Why? They were patrolling, not raiding. What happened out there?" Cormac stood up, his brow knotted in consternation. There was no reason for prisoners to have been taken.

"Please come, Father. You need to see this."

****

Cormac came out into the courtyard, the bright blue sky forcing him to squint. His eyes were tired from writing. A small group of about twelve men, women, and children were huddled together, their hands were bound behind their backs, Cormac noted. They would have been stripped of their weapons, but they wore no armor and did not have the hardened faces of warriors. "Who are these people?" Cormac asked.

"Prisoners, my King. From across our borders," came a voice from a face he did not recognize.

"Ceallach. Who addresses me?"

"I am—"

"Ceallach," Cormac interrupted the man's response, raising his voice. "Who addresses me?"

"Father, this is Aonach. He led these men in my stead."

"You picked him?" the King asked.

"I did not."

"Aonach…" Cormac said quietly.

"My King?" asked Aonach, a small man with a flat nose which looked like it had been broken many times.

"Where were these prisoners taken from?"

"An Linn Beag, my King."

"An Linn Beag. Leinster," Cormac said, crouching next to one of the prisoners, a woman of about twenty years. He raised her chin gently and gazed into her fearful wide eyes as he spoke, "You took these people from Leinster."

"They will make valuable slaves, my Lord. You will fetch a good price," replied Aonach. He pulled one of the women to her feet and continued, "The men are strong and the women are ripe."

"The women are ripe," Cormac said, as he stood.

"And the children too," Aonach replied.

At this, Cormac stiffened, "You have tried them?" he asked, raising an eyebrow.

"I have not, my King. I would not," Aonach stammered.

"But you said they are ripe," Cormac pressed.

"I mean, I would not try them without permission, my King," he stammered.

"Permission from me, Aonach?" Cormac turned to face him, looking him directly in the eye.

"Yes, my King. I would not do such a thing without your permission."

"But you would do such a thing?" Cormac asked. "This woman is bleeding between her legs. It seems you could not wait for my permission."

Aonach remained silent. His palms were sweating. What was this, he thought to himself. Why was he being pressed so hard for bringing slaves? "Yes, I used the woman, but…" he trailed off, unsure what he was to say.

"It's alright, Aonach. It's alright," Cormac reassured him. "We'll have this worked out shortly. Who picked this man to lead the patrol?"

"Matudan, Father," Ceallach spoke up.

"Send for him," the King replied. "Immediately."

"My King, if I have offended you—" Aonach started.

"Kneel," Cormac shouted. He cut him off with such sudden fury that everyone fell silent and looked to the ground.

"My King," Aonach was still confused.

"On your knees, dog," Cormac shouted at him, as Matudan arrived in the courtyard, his bald head shone in the sun.

"Matudan," Cormac said, his voice regained some composure.

"Yes, my King," the warrior replied.

"Aonach is your man?"

"He is, my Lord."

"He raided across the border and took prisoners. You gave him permission to do this?"

"I gave him leave to lead the patrol with his own foresight," Matudan replied. He sensed the delicate atmosphere and threaded lightly, "If he has acted out of favor, then I take responsibility."

Cormac turned to Matudan, an eyebrow raised, "You would take responsibility for the ravage of the innocent, Matudan? For this man?" He raised a finger, "Think carefully here before you answer, Matudan. You are valuable to be, but not indispensable. He condones the rape of women and children. Do you take responsibility for that?"

"My King, I—" Matudan stammered.

"Father," Ceallach broke in, hoping to diffuse the situation.

"Matudan," Cormac said, ignoring his son. "Are you a Christian?"

"I am," replied Matudan, a Christian by birth maybe, but he did not practice any religion or hold any God dear to his heart.

"Do you condone the rape of women and children?" Cormac continued.

"I do not, my Lord," Matudan replied.

"I see," Cormac lowered his gaze and closed his eyes a moment. How he wished not to be a King at times like this. "Kill this man," he said.

"Father," Ceallach tried once more.

"Do not argue with me on this, Ceallach," Cormac said, raising his forefinger, red in the face. "Matudan. Do not delay. It will not bode well for you."

This was a warning not to be taken lightly, Matudan knew. Cormac was a man of peace, and this was extreme. He knew better than to argue.

"Have these people fed and cleaned. I will be in the chapel." With that, he left.

The captives were fed and watered as instructed, and Aonach was brought outside the castle walls, kicking and screaming, and hung by the neck until he turned blue and died, his bloated corpse hung there for many days, as the crows feasted, as a reminder of what would happen to those who took pleasure from the mistreatment of the innocent. Or those, who would take advantage of the spoils of war, like himself, Matudan thought, as he cut down the foul-smelling remains seven days later. He had indulged in the spoils of war many times and could have ended up hanging from a tree himself, swaying in the wind.

****

Chapter Six

Flaithbertach pushed his curragh into the salty sea off the mainland, sending his two remaining brothers to give word to Cormac of what had happened, after which they would make the long journey to the monastery at Iona, where they had come from two years before.

Flaithbertach sailed north along the coast for two days before putting in at a remote coastal community in the Kingdom of Connaught, where he would find the one he was looking for.

The sky was a dark blue when he arrived, with streaks of purple cloud saluting the setting sun, signaling the coming of dawn. He had brought his curragh upriver through the sandy shores to drag it up the muddy bank, his grubby abbot's robes were still black from ash, his hair long and tossed, and beard unkempt. He looked every bit the weary traveler he felt.

Wary farmers' eyes peered out through the mud huts in the fading light, trying to decide if this man was friend or foe. None would remember him, he knew. Flaithbertach had left this place many years ago.

He pulled his curragh up onto a stony shore and gathered some sticks. He lit a small fire before falling asleep under a grizzled old tree. The locals went to bed, deciding this lone stranger wasn't a Viking or a cattle raider.

The light of the new day revealed a few huts of wood with straw roofs. Smoke rose through a hole in the center, and the smell of cooking and the calls of sheep brought Flaithbertach to his senses. The sun was high in the sky, he had slept late. Half a day's walk lay ahead of him if he couldn't find a horse, and he wanted to arrive before nightfall.

The huts surrounded a larger log building, home to the local representative of the King of Connaught. A donkey path lead eastward, inland to where the last remnants of pagan Ireland resided. Small pockets of those who refused to convert and still worshiped the old Gods. These people were a dying breed, as the world gave way to the golden age of Christianity.

The path brought him through the forest, the canopy overhead becoming thicker as he ventured deeper, searching for the ancient place he remembered from his childhood.

Flaithbertach was born in these parts and grew up here until he was sent to fight, to pay a debt his father could not afford.

He sought council from one of the pagan priests of the old Gods. If he was still here, that is.

As he moved through the gloom of the forest, shining white skulls mounted on stakes stared back at him through hollow, black eyes. They did not grin back at him like the blackened skulls from the chapel, as their lower jaws were missing, but he could feel their judgment as he passed. Who knows how long these silent sentries had watched this trail?

He would drive the nailed God from this land and build a pagan nation, unified through worship and a hatred of outsiders. Flaithbertach Mac Imnain was no longer Abbot of Innis Caithigh, but the next pagan King in Ireland.

Chapter Seven

Cormac found himself in the stone beehive hut in front of the pale-faced man yet again. He sat. He was calmer this time. It was dark when he reached the top of the steps to pass through the stone wall and entered the hut as before. The rain fell, battering the lonely island. *Who was coming?* he thought. *The men on the armored horses?* He knew now that he could think this over for as long as he wanted. He could sit here until the end of time, pondering his next question. He needed to ask the right question. Who was coming?

"What must I do?" he finally asked. He did not care who it was that would come. He would defeat them. He would protect his land and people.

"You must bring peace," came the answer as quickly as before. "You must bring peace and unite your island. Make peace with the Norsemen. Make peace with the ancient Kings and the High Kings. Stand united as one kingdom and you will prepare your descendants for what is coming. Only together can you defeat them. Only together can you preserve your true nature and come out of this unbroken. The Norsemen can be powerful allies. Welcome them and use them as such. Share your island with them and stand together to break the ones who will come."

Cormac sat, thinking. He stared at the messenger, unsure what to say when he felt himself being pulled back to the waking world as he had each time. The pale man was speaking again, but it was fading, "Beware of the serpent who falls."

****

She loved him. She was not attracted to him physically, but she loved him. She loved his wisdom, his calmness, his fairness, his respect. He truly was a great man and a great King.

"What do great men dream of?" she asked him, turning onto her side to look him in the eye.

"Peace," he said. "I don't know about great men, but I dream of peace." He closed his eyes and thought of the place he grew up in. He could almost see the white clouds rolling past. White clouds always reminded him of being a child. He would lie on the grass, staring at the sky, thinking about his lessons, thinking about God, thinking about the world outside his world. He was privileged enough, at a young age, to have access to books and writing materials. He read everything. There was no written history of the land in which he lived, so he would ask the old men all about the stories of their lives and their grandfathers and those before them. He would write all the stories down and the monks would complain that he was wasting their writing material. Let the past be, they would say.

Cormac saw the past as a gateway to the future. What had happened, paved the way for what was to come. They could learn from it.

He studied words, languages, numbers, and potions, and he read about battles. Great battles in the past. The Romans, when they had outposts across the water. He read about the tribes who had come from the east, he read about the Norsemen, never thinking that they would eventually become part of everyday life. He learned how to govern. He saw how it could be done. How it should be done, showing respect to all.

He sat up in his bed, his old back was stiff. "Peace, Gormfhlaith," he said again. "It can happen, you know," he said, as he rubbed his face vigorously, then stood to stretch.

"But we have peace, my King. You and I saw to that."

"You must remember to call me by my name. My name is Cormac. There are no formalities here," his reprimand was said in kindness and he smiled.

She saw tiredness in that smile. Weariness in the eyes. She smiled back, hiding her worry about his health.

"Yes, we have peace here. For now. But I'm thinking bigger." He crossed the room and pulled a cloak over his old naked body, and sat at his writing table, taking out his feathered quill and some ink, "I mean everywhere." He dipped his pen and began to write. He wrote his thoughts every morning. An expensive habit, but an essential habit, he told her. To understand one's world, you must understand yourself. And to do that, you need to make sense of your innermost thoughts.

"I aim to bring peace, Gormfhlaith."

"I don't understand," she said. "You already did. By marrying me, you guaranteed peace for decades."

"No," he said again. Putting down the quill, he looked at her. There was so much she didn't understand. So much she would learn, "I'm talking about the island. The entire island. I have made peace with your father and with Ceirbeall, and now, I aim to make peace with the Norsemen. I aim to unite this island."

She stared at him. Peace with the Norsemen. Pagan killers and rapists of women. "The Norsemen," she repeated.

"The Norsemen," he replied. "In fact, I write to their King in the east now. It is the only way."

"Many people hate them. They will not like it. Flaithbertach hates them."

"Flaithbertach need not worry himself so much about my affairs. Besides, he need not know. Not yet, at least." He continued to write and remained silent for a long time, as the morning sun rose outside, the first rays hit the floor through the narrow window and grew longer as he wrote.

Gormfhlaith got out of her bed and dressed after drinking off a swig of wine which was at her bedside. She kissed him and left him in peace, with his letters and his dreams of peace. He was no fool, she knew. He would not attempt this if he did not believe it could be done.

He continued writing long into the afternoon, bent over his page like an aged, white beetle. He needed the right words. He needed to find common ground with these men. There were many factions of Norsemen spread throughout the land and they burned and destroyed in their wake. Their way was the sword. Peace had a price. Peace had to be fought for. But not on his land. Not on his island. He would make peace with all those within the border of the sea.

He would offer them his sword and his land. To live side by side, to draw blood together and die fighting for each other, not against each other.

He finished his letter and summoned his foster sons and Finnan. No one else would hear of this. Not now, at least.

Chapter Eight

Flaithbertach sat quietly, enjoying his ale. "What do you make of it?" he asked Aodh. Aodh, foster son to the King and foster brother to Ceallach came to Thomand when he was a boy. He was eighteen years old.

"Make of what?" the young man asked.

"The King's plan."

"What plan?" replied the youth, feigning ignorance. He had been told to discuss the King's plans with nobody outside of Finnan, Ceallach, and the King.

"The plan you were discussing this morning," Flaithbertach returned, smiling.

"I didn't know you knew."

"Aodh, I'm your father's closest advisor," the monk replied. "Now, what do you make of it?"

"It's not my place to judge."

"Why?" asked the abbot. He put down his cup and sat back. Flaithbertach always listened to Aodh. He always made him feel at ease when nobody else seemed to respect him.

"He's the King," Aodh replied. "Who am I to question him?" Many people were wary of Flaithbertach, but Aodh felt like he could talk to him.

"You can have an opinion, my young friend," Flaithbertach encouraged him. "In fact, you must," he emphasized, "You must have an opinion. If you're ever to make a good leader, you must question everything."

Aodh shook his head, "I can't question the King, Flaithbertach." His voice shook a little. They were outside the castle grounds, sharing ale. Aodh could feel his face warm despite the breeze.

"You can, and you will." The monk was sitting cross-legged against an old oak tree. Its gnarled trunk framed his strong body. "In time, I suppose. Anyway, what do you make of it?" he pressed.

"'Tis madness." Aodh admitted, finding some confidence in his friend's assurances. "Madness," he said again, and shook his head.

"Ha-ha," Flaithbertach laughed out loud, ale dribbled down his black beard. He wiped it on his sleeve, "That's more like it." They drank together on occasion, Flaithbertach listened to the young man's problems and offered advice where he could. "Tell it like it is, then," he said, and took another mouthful. "Why do you think it is mad?" Flaithbertach passed him the leather bag of ale.

"Peace," said the youth, as he took another mouthful. It loosened his tongue. He liked that. "Mad. There is no peace. There can't be. With them? Mad," he went on.

With who, thought Flaithbertach.

"I feel the same," he said, "but the King knows best. We must look out for him all the same, Aodh. Do you think there is danger?"

Aodh thought about it and took a swig before answering. "Yes," he said after some thought, "There is." He spat to one side, "He means to visit them, you know. Or send one of us. Me or Ceallach to treat with them. Into the lion's den."

Meet with who, and where, thought Flaithbertach. He didn't like where this was going.

"On neutral ground?" he asked. "Holy ground maybe? Blood will not be spilled on holy ground," he volunteered.

"Pagans don't care about spilling blood on holy ground, Flaithbertach," Aodh said.

Pagans, thought Flaithbertach. He meant to offer peace to the Norsemen. That, Flaithbertach resolved, was something he would never allow to happen.

"That's true," he whispered. "We will see."

****

The two men sat in darkness and faced each other across a small table, the gentle candlelight flickered across their faces. The wind howled outside, the summer storms had come.

Cormac pulled his great fleece tighter around him as he concentrated on his friend's impenetrable face. He could not make out his thoughts through the heavy wooden door to Flaithbertach's mind. Cormac was always easy to read. He prided himself in being honest and transparent. One must be transparent in order to gain trust. One must be trusted in order to lead and to teach. Cormac Mac Cuileneann was both a leader and a teacher.

The man sitting across from him had entered into the same religious vein as Cormac. He was however a different man, Cormac knew, as he considered

48

his friend. Though he could not guess at his thoughts, he knew that hard, scarred face covered a scarred mind.

"I'll get that fire going, my Lord. It's a bad night out there. The wind is howling and the rain is coming down heavy, and I thank God I'm under your roof tonight and not out in the fields."

"Thank you, Desmond," Cormac replied to his servant. Cormac was always courteous to those around him. It was the way of God and the way for a King to lead and treat those under his protection.

"Make your move, my King," Flaithbertach said calmly, as Desmond, on hands and knees, started to pack some logs in the fire ring in the middle of the room. "You've been sitting staring at me for an age. You'll not find answers on my face, but on the board before you," Flaithbertach continued, not letting his impatience show through his words. Keep your mask on, he always said. Nobody should ever see the real you.

They would see the real Flaithbertach however. He would come out. Not long now.

The fire started to smoke a little until it caught flame, shedding more light on the board in front of them, as Cormac reached down and lifted a piece to make his move.

"What are your thoughts on Finnan?" Cormac asked, switching to Latin. Although he trusted his servant some conversations were best kept between the fighting men.

"Why do you ask, my King?" Flaithbertach replied in Latin.

Cormac sat in silence for a minute and thought on it. Finnan was one of his best warriors. Strong. Decisive.

"I'm thinking he should lead. He is a great warrior, but quick to anger. Can he keep his head when it comes down to it?"

"Can he keep his head?" Flaithbertach mused, as he placed his piece. He stood from their game and walked to the table behind them, his back to Cormac.

"He can be trusted, my King," Flaithbertach responded, turning from the table, slipping his hand underneath his cloak, unnoticed. He had what he had come for, "He is quick to anger, but with intelligence beyond any soldier I have seen."

Cormac sat, eyes closed, considering. He could feel the warmth of the fire now and he was glad of it. He felt old and weary. He had never asked for the life of a King. He only ever wished to lead a holy life in service to God and fill himself with the riches of the mind to share with the world.

"I'm tired, Flaithbertach," he switched back to their native Gaelic. "I'm going to bed."

"God be with you, my King."

"And with you, Flaithbertach," Cormac said, as the younger man slipped out.

As Cormac turned, his eye was drawn to their game. He was caught. He had been beaten and had not even noticed.

****

Flaithbertach sat on a wooden stool in his dark lodgings, at a small table, staring at the parchment before him, considering what he was about to do. From here, there was no turning back. He picked up his quill in his right hand, an ornate, swan quill, a gift from brother, Edmund, when he was appointed abbot.

The wind rose and howled outside, as he rolled the quill back and forth between his thumb and forefinger, contemplating. "No turning back," he muttered quietly to himself.

He sat in the gloomy darkness, listening to the hiss of rain as it poured down. He reached forward and dipped the quill into the black ink and began to write. Bent over the small table like an old crooked branch, scratching at the parchment in front of him. He was skilled in the art of writing, as any abbot should be. He drafted it carefully, addressing the Holy Father in Rome himself.

The candle was burning low as he had finished. He laid the quill on the table and read over the contents of what he had written. Latin. He knew Matudan was schooled in Latin. This would work. It was simple.

He stood from his stool and rolled the parchment tightly. Holding the red wax stick to the candle, he melted it until a small drop of red fell from its tip, mixing with the white wax of the candle below. He reached under his cloak and pulled out the seal which he had taken from Cormac. With one last pause, he bonded the rolled parchment closed and marked the wax with Cormac's seal, turned, and stepped out into the stormy night.

****

Matudan woke to the sound of thunder cracking through the night, the hiss of rain outside and the howl of the wind. He sat up to clear his head. He had been dreaming of a figure, a dark figure. He looked around in the gloom but could see nothing, save the dark shapes of the sleeping men around him. The room stank from each end of the sleeping soldiers, deep in a drunken slumber.

"Matudan," came a voice through the darkness. "Matudan, wake up, we must speak."

"I'm awake," he replied. "Who comes to me in the dark of night to speak? Show yourself."

A shape glided silently toward him through the gloom from the doorway.

"It's Flaithbertach. We must speak in private. It's about tomorrow," he whispered in Latin, fearing any of the other soldiers might overhear them. "Take a walk with me. It is important," he hissed.

Matudan knew Flaithbertach was the King's closest friend and advisor, but knew little else of the man. He cursed as he threw on a cloak and followed the abbot out into the rain.

"What is so important that it couldn't wait until tomorrow and that you must drag me out into this piss night?"

"I have important information for you," replied Flaithbertach, as he turned to face Matudan.

"What in the hell could—"

"Hush, fool," Flaithbertach interrupted. Matudan said nothing, for he knew the black monk's reputation. "The King has dispatched a messenger to Rome," Flaithbertach continued.

"What of it?" the warrior demanded, growing cold in the rain. "Speak on, man. It's wet out."

"You will need to see the contents of that letter, Matudan," Flaithbertach whispered.

"Why?" insisted the bald warrior, as he pulled his cloak tighter around him. They stopped under the gable of the building to shelter from the rain.

"You will see when you read it," answered the monk, "but it is something you must see at any cost. Any cost, Matudan," he said again, grabbing Matudan's arm. "Any cost."

"What are you suggesting, monk?" Matudan asked, as he pulled his arm free. The rain pelted down on top of them.

"I am suggesting you meet the messenger in the morning, far enough from here to give you privacy and convince him however you wish, to let you read that letter and do what you will with the information."

"It is raining, monk, I'm going back to bed," Matudan said, but as he turned, he caught something in the monk's eye. A darkness. A light maybe? He didn't know. Something that convinced him he should see that letter. The monk just stared back at him. Matudan turned and left.

****

Matudan was nervous as he rode. He eyed the messenger ahead of him. The storm the night before had blown off and the morning was clear, however, he had gotten little sleep since his discussion with Flaithbertach.

He rode on in silence, a lone wolf howled in the distance. It wouldn't bother the two of them on horses. Wolves were scarce this close to the settlements.

"Matudan, I thank you for volunteering to escort me," said Colm cheerfully. He was a short, happy monk who had come through Thomand recently on route to Rome. The journey ahead of him would take months. "How far to the river?" he asked.

"Not long," replied Matudan. "Not long. The boat will take you southwest along the coast," he continued, squinting at the glare of the sunlight through the branches. This path was little used and overgrown. "Then south and east along the coast until you can cross the sea – I haven't heard of any Norse attacks recently."

"No," replied the messenger. "We go with God. We will be safe."

"God will kill the Norsemen for you, will he?" laughed Matudan, as he slowed down and dismounted.

"Why are you stopping?" asked Colm.

"I need to take a piss and I advise you to do the same, we won't be stopping again."

"I thought you said we were close," replied the fair-haired messenger as he dismounted.

He wandered over close to where Matudan stood to relieve himself.

"What's in the letter?" asked Matudan, as he drained himself over the lush green ferns of the thick forest. "Why is it so urgent?"

"The letter is between the King and the Holy Father, and is no business of mine or yours," the fat monk said.

It was worth a try. He had hoped it wouldn't come to this, but he had to read that letter. He had to know what was so important.

"Come, we must move," he said, and put his left hand on the messenger's shoulder as they walked toward the horses. With the ease of a hardened warrior, he unhooked his axe with his right hand and raised it as he turned the messenger to face him. Surprise was all that showed as the axe came down on his face. A wet thud, his knees jerked sporadically in a dance before he dropped to the ground, a lifeless lump.

He pulled his axe free and rummaged under the cloak. He hoped he had not killed this man for nothing. There it was, under the seal of the King. As he began to read, he understood how this affected him personally, but why did the mad monk bring it to his attention?

52

Under the seal of Cormac, King of Munster, was a written oath, to use all the spoils of war and the wealth of his Kingdom for the glory of Christ, to spread the word of God throughout this island. His soldiers were men of God and had no love for plunder or gold, and above all, loved and worshiped Christ.

****

The war council had been gathered.

It was noon on July 25, 908, and the sun was shining outside the halls of Thomand. Men had come from all corners of Munster to hear what their King had to say. A table had been set in the great hall to seat all those required. Specific places were set for Cormac, the King, Flaithbertach and Finnan, his closest advisors, Aodh and Ceallach, his foster sons.

Other than that, people filled in one by one. The King would arrive at noon and the council would commence. Meonach sat quietly by the right hand of Cormac's seat, usually reserved for Flaithbertach, but the priest, Meonach, had provided important advice to the King before this meeting.

Men were still coming in, taking their seats, and exchanging words of greeting with one another. Fogartach, son of Suibne, King of Ciarraige, arrived, looking splendid, with a great bearskin cloak draped over his shoulders. Fogartach was renowned for great knowledge in philosophy and theology, and he was considered one of the most learned men in Munster.

He was followed by Aillill, son of Eogan, who, as if to outdo Fogartach, wore a great bear cape also, but of the most exquisite white fur anyone had ever seen. Surely plundered from the Vikings or a gift from them, who knew.

Then came Cormac, King of Dessi, Dubucan, King of Fir Mairge, and Cenn Faelad, who was in exile in Munster, but who had served Cormac loyally in the past. Though not native to these lands, he was a welcome warrior and advisor.

Matudan and Maol Muid arrived together as usual, for the two were inseparable, followed by Flaithbertach. A dark cloud hung over the monk since the business with the Vikings in Innis Caithigh. No doubt this would be up for discussion at the council.

Dud Da Baireann, Congall, and Catharnach, all took their seats, followed by Federach who entered with Finnan. Finnan's piercing blue eyes scanned the room and the faces, taking in as much information as he could in as little time as possible, always expecting trouble. He sat himself beside Flaithbertach.

Last to arrive before King Cormac were Aed, King of Ui Liathain, and Domhnall, King of Dun Cerma.

Conversation buzzed around the table as the men spoke about what they thought would be up for discussion. Some spoke about Cormac. How he was an aged King not getting any younger. "Age begets wisdom," some interjected on his part. Elders were respected in Gaelic Ireland and always had been. The very old had played an important part in the pre-Christian Gaelic culture. Pope Leo himself was the same age as Cormac, and he was, in a sense, the leader of the world.

Silence fell as the King entered. He looked splendid in his golden crown, a simple decorated band which wrapped around his forehead, joined at each end by a wolf's head, with his jaws around a deer's neck.

It was said that Cormac had a particular love for wild animals, especially wolves, in which he saw a great intelligence. He called them dogs who preferred the company of other dogs rather than men.

Cormac took his seat between Meonach and Finnan, and all remained silent as they waited for him to speak.

The King cleared his throat. "My friends, we live in dangerous and changing times. I will get to the point," he said, as he surveyed the faces around him. His white beard gave away his age, but also showed wisdom in his face.

"The Norsemen constantly attack us and have already settled our island."

"We must attack them," came a voice from the back.

"Drive them out," came another.

Cormac held up a thin hand for silence. He was weary and he felt it in his bones. His mind was tired from endless hours of debate and conversation with Meonach regarding his dreams. Beware the serpent who falls... The pale-faced man's words had haunted Cormac, but neither him nor Meonach could find meaning in them. He was, however, certain of the course of action.

"What we must do is make ourselves strong," Cormac countered.

Somber, thoughtful faces looked back at him.

"An enemy is coming. This, I have seen. An enemy that the kingdom of Munster cannot hope to defeat."

"My King," interjected Flaithbertach, "which enemy do you speak of? We have all seen the enemy. We have all felt their wrath and we know what we must do."

"The King is speaking," Finnan said. "Let him finish."

Cormac patted Finnan gently on the arm and turned to Flaithbertach, directing his words at him, for he knew Flaithbertach would be the hardest one to convince, "Flaithbertach, I have seen it in my dreams. The enemy is coming.

They will come in great ships, and in numbers greater than any enemy force we have ever seen."

His words rang throughout the hall. These men were both religious and superstitious. But they were also intelligent and practical men, and asking them to believe in a dream may have been a stretch too far.

"We must unite. We need all the help we can get. We need Flan Sinna. We need Ceirbeall, Osraigh, and Connaught. We need them all. And Flaithbertach, please hear me, we need the Norsemen in the south and the Norsemen in the east. They can be powerful allies. They are already here and they are not leaving."

He sat back in his chair and surveyed the faces around him, trying to gage their reactions. Finnan sat back, also looking around for a reaction. Whether the King believed what he was saying or if this was an elaborate ploy to bring peace to this war-ravaged land, he did not know. Cormac was a lover and advocate of peace, and would never fight if it could be avoided.

It was Aillill of the white bearskin who spoke first, "My King, I would follow you to the ends of the earth, but what makes you think these Norsemen can be trusted? Or our own neighbors, for that matter?"

"And when are these enemies coming?" asked Fogartach.

"And who are they?" chimed in Dubucan.

Cormac expected this. He knew they could not just support his decision based on a dream. Flaithbertach, he noticed, remained silent.

"We do not know when they will come," said Meonach. Meonach was deeply respected and Cormac had needed his help in interpreting the dreams. "But mark my words, they are coming from the east."

"Saxons," shouted Cenn Faelad. "My own people. They are even busier than we are with the Norsemen. They cannot be a threat."

"Not the Saxons," said Cormac, as he shook his head. "They will ride over the Saxons on great, armored horses and then sneak into our lands and tear our island apart. We must unite and become strong together. It is the only way."

And so the discussion and debate went on long into the afternoon, and into the evening, and again reconvened the next day. Men spoke and Kings spoke, and they argued and they counterargued. Some pushed for war, others were willing to try peace, but in the end, the decision was Cormac's and Cormac's alone, and his mind was made up.

He would send envoys north and east, to all corners and kingdoms of the island. Flaithbertach, he would send to the Vikings in Dublin. Flaithbertach, Cormac thought, the one who had been wronged most by the Norsemen, would be the best one to show them they were willing to make peace. He would need to convince Flaithbertach of the necessity of his plan.

And with that, the war council was finished and for the first time, Cormac had a genuine hope of peace for the entire island.

****

It was three days after the war council before the monk and the bald, old warrior had a chance to meet and discuss the findings of the letter in the dead of night.

"You got the letter then?" Flaithbertach hissed through the dark.

"I did," Matudan replied. It was not raining tonight, which he was grateful for.

"You have the wits to be able to read it?" Flaithbertach pressed.

"I'm not feeble-minded, monk, of course I can read it," Matudan said, eager to get to the point.

"What did you make of it?" whispered the monk.

"I had to read it twice to believe it. He means to pledge all our bloody plunder to the Pope," he said. "Some fat fool across the sea?" Matudan said. "What of his men? How did you know?"

"He discussed it with me. Shh. Someone approaches. Yes," he said, changing the subject. "The evening is damp. More rain to come, I think," he waffled, as a soldier passed. They stood on the walkway atop the castle walls, looking out on the land below. Flaithbertach could see the distant fires of camps and farms burning in the distance. He paused to allow the soldier to pass, "What did you make of it?"

"We can't have it," said Matudan.

"So what will you do about it?"

"Do about it? Me?" Matudan asked. "What the hell did you have me get the bloody letter for? I thought you had something going?"

"I see," said Flaithbertach. "Well, what would you do about it then, if you were his closest ear?"

"I'd change his mind. That's what I'd do. Have a good stern word in his ear."

"A good stern word," Flaithbertach repeated, breathing the cold night air deep. "In the King's ear," he sighed.

"Yes," agreed Matudan.

"Yes," repeated Flaithbertach. "Good stern words don't work with Kings, Matudan."

"Well, what then?" asked the warrior.

"You tell me."

"No. I won't. I told you," said Matudan, raising his voice. "What are you getting at, Flaithbertach?"

"Keep your voice down," Flaithbertach whispered. "You are a soldier," he went on.

"I am. Speak plain, man. Get on with it," Matudan said, calmer now.

"You must be paid to do your job."

"I must," he agreed. "We all must be paid. We need to eat and have comforts of some sort."

"Well, you're not going to be paid. Not by your King, anyway. So, what will you do?" Flaithbertach pressed.

"Fight for someone else?" Matudan volunteered.

"Who?" Flaithbertach asked. "Ceirbeall? Flan Sinna?" he suggested. "Sell your sword? You would leave your home?"

"No. I wouldn't."

"No, of course you wouldn't," the monk whispered through the cold air. "You stay."

"Stay?" Matudan questioned.

"Stay," repeated Flaithbertach, feeding Matudan's own words back to him, convincing him. He had not realized this would be so tedious.

"And then what?" the warrior asked, scratching his chin. "You said yourself, stern words are no good."

"You stay," Flaithbertach whispered quickly, his breath fogged in the cool, spring air. "And you fight and you earn your keep as a soldier. And when the time comes, you raid with your King and reap the profits of flesh, gold, and silver."

Matudan dismissed Flaithbertach with a wave of his hand, "Our King executes men for taking profits of the flesh and he has just promised his gold and silver to Rome."

"You're not getting it, fool," Flaithbertach said.

Matudan turned to face him, "Careful, monk, it's a long way to the bottom of the wall."

"What if things were different? Would that satisfy you? Raid the borders. Reap the profits," Flaithbertach went on.

"It would. Yes. It would. But our King won't allow it."

"So, what do we need?"

Silence followed as Matudan considered, then something struck him. Something, he had never dared think about, "We need a new King."

"Ha-ha-ha. There we are. I knew you weren't stupid," said Flaithbertach. "We will speak again." He turned to walk away, but paused after a step, "Matudan?"

"Yes…"

"If you ever threaten me again, I'll cut your tongue out and make you eat it." He walked into the gloom and disappeared.

****

Flaithbertach had sailed southeast and put into land, to camp on a deserted beach in the driving rain. He was accompanied by Maol Muid, Matudan, and his friend, Aodh, the uncertain young foster son to the King. They wore warriors' clothes, leather armor, and carried weapons. They were accompanied by a force of fourteen men and three horses.

His mood was dark and had been, since his King had put forth this venture to him. The old fool had put the final nail in the coffin for him. Peace with the Norsemen. Peace with creatures who had murdered his brothers. *Maybe so,* he thought, but on his terms. Not Cormac's.

"We will make camp up off the beach. Make the boat secure or we'll never get back," Flaithbertach ordered. He seemed more like the warrior of old now, rather than the abbot of recent years, "Ready the horses. We leave immediately. Aodh, I leave you in charge of the camp and our goods. Maol Muid, Matudan, and I will go treat with the Norsemen."

Maol Muid was Matudan's right-hand man. They were inseparable.

Aodh was chuffed with this task. He had been in battle before, but never had taken charge of men and he eagerly set about making the place ready, setting up tents, digging trenches, setting scouts, and a perimeter. He was learned in the ways of war. And now, he had a chance to put it into practice.

Flaithbertach smiled to himself at the youth's progress, as he mounted up and rode off into the midmorning sun with his two companions. "If I'm not back by noon tomorrow, then we are likely dead and your father's plan has failed. Head back," he told the younger man.

"I'll not leave you," Aodh had argued.

Flaithbertach smiled and clapped him on the shoulder, "You will and you must. But we will return. We will promise the Norsemen gold and silver, and the prospect of land in which they can live in peace. We will be back."

"You will," said Aodh.

"Yes," Flaithbertach replied, "but," he paused, "if not…you know what to do. And no argument." He smiled and left.

Aodh liked Flaithbertach. He had always been good to him. He did not know where Finnan's unfounded suspicion of the monk had come from. He watched the three figures ride west from the lonely open stretch of land on which they had beached their boat. "God bless and good luck," he whispered.

Then, in a louder voice, "Back to work, let's keep ourselves busy while we wait, I want this camp ready and breakfast, lunch, and dinner caught. Hunting parties, you, you, and you." The men looked at him dubiously, thinking about the dried meat and bread they had brought with them, and Aodh realized they were ignoring him. "Now," he shouted with a confidence he didn't feel. They looked at each other before rising to set about their tasks.

****

By sundown, a small camp was set up, a fire burned, with rabbit and pheasant roasting over it. Scouting parties he had sent out reported nothing out of the ordinary. They spoke to a farmer in the area and found that the Norsemen were about a four-hour ride away and had given little trouble since they arrived last year.

"They tend to stick to bigger targets and leave the little fellows like me alone," he had said through a toothless grin. "Maybe they'll come for you and your boys though, strangers like you fellows roving around our parts," he said, as he shielded his eyes from the sun. The scouts left him be and he went back about his business.

The night was uneventful. The men drank a little but not too much. They were in enemy territory and needed their wits about them. Aodh did not indulge. He couldn't handle it at the best of times. The rain stopped and he slept for a few hours, rising as the fire died down to make a round of the night guards and see if anything was afoot.

"Nothing here," he was told. "You might as well go back to sleep."

"No," he said to the man. He didn't know his name. "You go to sleep, I'll take your shift." He was used to doing a soldier's work anyway. The man accepted and left him in the dark without a word. He thought about the possibilities of what they were trying to do, as he sat in the darkness, his back to the crackling fire behind him. There was no moon. It was pitch black out there. He would see any lanterns approach. They had a good view all around. Nobody could be out here without a torch; therefore, nobody could sneak up on them.

He watched as a faint light flickered in the distance. He guessed it was the fire from the farm his scouts had come across. Other than that, there was nothing. No life. The silence was only broken by the hoot of an owl and the whisper of the guard who had come to relieve him shortly before dawn. He would sleep for a short while now, after he inspected their cargo, a small amount of gold and silver they had taken with them to convince the Norsemen of their good intentions. Some of it had already gone into the night with the three riders.

******

The air of the soldiers in the dawn was different. They accepted Aodh's authority and carried out his tasks without hesitation. The tide was on its way in and their boat began to float back up when riders were spotted in the distance.

"They bear Flaithbertach's flag," the man on guard called. Aodh could not see the flag, his eyesight was poor and he cursed as he asked how many were there.

"Eight or nine, all mounted," one of the guards shouted back.

"Be ready, we don't want any surprises. They could have killed our men and are coming to take our silver. Weapons in hand," he shouted.

An unnecessary precaution, as Flaithbertach rode in to camp, he slowed and dismounted, with six other horsemen. Aodh and his men had never seen the Norsemen before. All of them were bearded, with light hair of red and yellow and brown and pale-blue eyes. They carried round shields, much like the Gaelic men, with a metal boss in the middle and seemed to favor axes over swords.

They wore heavy animal skins, some over their shoulders and some on their chests, and one man had a human jawbone hanging from his neck, gleaming white in the morning sun. Their skin was tattooed in a dark blue ink of varying design on their arms, their faces, and god knows where else.

They dismounted and looked about warily. "These men are our friends," Flaithbertach announced. "This is Canute," he gestured to the one with the jawbone, "son of Torgny. Torgny is open to discussions of peace." He spoke to Canute in a language alien to Aodh, but he heard his own name and the name of his foster father in the exchange. He guessed it was an introduction, and nodded to the Norseman.

The Norseman nodded and spoke to Flaithbertach again.

"Aodh, have your men bring the gold chest," he said. It pleased Aodh that Flaithbertach respected his authority in front of the men.

The gold and silver were exchanged and the Norsemen rode away, both parties were uncertain if a true alliance had been achieved, but it was a start as Flaithbertach had told Aodh.

******

60

The halls of Thomand were dark for it was late. Two men sat over a pitcher of ale in the kitchen.

"What did you make of it?" Matudan asked, his voice muffled slightly by the dagger with which he navigated through his teeth with the skill of a master calligrapher.

"Make of what?" asked Finnan. He backed away from the stench emanating from Matudan's mouth.

"The plan. The visions. The mysterious invaders. Wooooo," he said, mimicking a phantom, as he waved the fingers of his free hand about Finnan's head.

"I am not here to question the King or discuss his plans," said Finnan, nobody else needed to know what he thought. Especially this ignorant beer-swigging lump in front of him.

"You speak plain enough," said Matudan, finding a sweet spot in his mouth to work on, rooting at one of the back teeth with his knife as he spoke through the blade. "Speak plain enough indeed," he continued, when Finnan made no reply. "But you give away nothing."

He observed the other man as the blade rummaged and rooted and twisted, his eyes slightly wide with concentration, which gave him a childlike look, as he waited for the Finnan to weigh in with something.

Matudan talked a lot but said little. He talked and drank and talked more, but then, he listened. He listened to men's stories and their thoughts and their opinions, as he continued to fill their goblets with ale or mead or sometimes wine, if he could get his hands on some. He listened and he remembered, and he assorted the information and sussed out where people's allegiances and ideals lay. He got the measure of men.

Finnan shifted his seat as the other man wrenched and pulled the blade. He imagined himself smacking the handle of the blade, pushing it straight through to the other side of the man's head and watching him collapse in a bleeding mess. *Best to leave that be*, he thought to himself. "Not sure what you want me to say, Matudan," he said, and took a drink from his ale.

"Light a candle there, will you?" Matudan called, as a slave passed by through the hallway. "We can't have ghosts like you sneaking about in the dark." he added. The slave was a blue man, a fear gorm, as they called them, though his skin was black as leather. An expensive purchase from a Saxon trader who had visited some years ago, taken from a land many miles away.

"Well, I just thought you would bloody well say something instead of sitting there like your tongue was cut out," with that, he twisted the blade sharply. There was a satisfying crunch as he dislodged a shitty, rotting tooth that had bothered him for weeks.

He spat the tooth and a mouthful of blood on the table in front of Finnan. "Good one," he shouted, as the blue man lit the candle, the dancing shadows retreated with the illumination.

Finnan ignored this and remained silent, as Matudan rinsed his mouth with ale and spat another mouthful on the floor this time, then downed the rest of his drink, the mixture of blood and ale satisfied him, the taste gave him the urge to spill someone else's blood as he stood and left the table.

****

A sharp wind tossed the cloaks of the figures who sat atop their horses, waiting patiently. The birds were beginning to wake and sing their songs as the dawn gave way to a bright morning, a rarity throughout this island of wind and rain.

The four riders, all hardened men, Flaithbertach, closest advisor to the King of Thomand, had left his abbot's robes behind, choosing to wear his battle armor instead. A round wooden shield hung across each man's back, the rising sun reflected on the metal boss in the center.

Flaithbertach was accompanied by Matudan, his loyalty bought with a simple letter and the promise of plunder in what would be a new era for the southwest. Matudan had chosen his most trusted friend and hardened warrior, Maol Muid, and three handpicked footmen who would obey Matudan's orders without question. They could not afford to have any more eyes involved in this exchange. One of the footmen stood with them, while the other two waited in the nearby forest lest there be trouble, or so they were told.

Flaithbertach did not expect any deception from the Leinstermen. He had not forgotten his previous conversation with Ceirbeall, but for now, the King of Leinster was honoring their trade proposal.

"Fuck this, I'm hungry," declared Matudan, as he dismounted and lead his spotted, gray mare to the closest tree to tether her. Broken branches littered the ground and, in a few minutes, Matudan had gathered a small pile and had a fire going, crackling through the morning air, rabbits lay beside it as he waited for the hot embers.

The men waited for an hour or so, eventually all dismounting to let their horses graze and sat by the fire, sharing the rabbit meat, more to pass the time than to satisfy hunger.

The footman, Seachnaill, who accompanied them, felt uncomfortable to be left with three men superior to him in rank, one of whom was the King's closest advisor. He was glad the conversation was sparse as he would have little to say

62

to these men. This worked both ways. He was just extra labor today and would be glad to get back to his family.

After some time, when they had eaten and Matudan had begun to slumber, lying back with his head resting on his shield, a call came from Maol Muid.

"Riders," he said.

Matudan shot up, like an animal pouncing, wide awake in an instant.

A good one to have on your side, thought Flaithbertach, as they moved forward to see six riders and a cart cresting the hill. A group of shaggy brown cows preceded the riders as they ambled down the hill, maybe twenty in total.

Maol Muid could spot the slow lumbering movement of a black bull making his way down with the group.

"The King has been generous," he said with a laugh, the joke not lost on Flaithbertach and Matudan.

The two groups came together and the cattle grazed, as the riders dismounted and faced each other. Though they had not met, Flaithbertach recognized their leader through his resemblance to his blood brother, Ceallach, who was fostered at Thomand.

"I am Flaithbertach, advisor to King Cormac, and you are Diarmuid, son of Ceirbeall. Your father has been generous."

"Yes, he has," replied Diarmuid, stepping forward. He was a muscular man, of about thirty-five years, and first born to the King of Leinster. He wore a sword by his side, which was fitting for the son of a King, but carried a spear in his right hand, which was unusual for a man of wealth. Rumor had it, he was the best spear fighter in the Kingdom of Leinster.

"Too generous if you ask me. I hope we see some of this returned to us in action."

"Indeed, you will," replied Flaithbertach, eying the four men behind Diarmuid, "You can be assured of that." Two of the men were of high rank, he could tell from their clothes and weapons. The other two were footmen, armed with spears.

"My men, Matudan and Maol Muid," said Flaithbertach, as he gestured either side of him.

Diarmuid in turn introduced Folloman and Tuathair, somber men, who, judging from their expressions, were not so enthusiastic about this exchange either.

Things moved on quickly after the initial pleasantries, if you would call them that. The cart and the cattle were left and the Leinstermen departed without much ceremony. The four men set to separating out the best of the weapons and loading them onto two of the grazing beasts. They kept spears in hand in case the bad-tempered bull turned on them as he would surely grow tired of their company. They would not kill such a valuable animal, but a hard smack on the nose would quickly demonstrate how things worked with his new owners.

After the Leinstermen departed, a bag of old, rusted blades which had been stored in the trees was thrown into the cart to replace what was left.

"When will we see you?" asked Matudan.

"Two or three days," replied Flaithbertach. "You will return to the King and let him judge the quality without your input. Maol Muid and I will take this one," he said, gesturing to Seachnaill. "You will tell Cormac I escorted Diarmuid back to Leinster, lest there be trouble. This is the beginning. Stay alert."

With that, they separated. Flaithbertach, Maol Muid, and Seachnaill, herding the black bull, the two beasts laden with weapons and the rest of the cattle.

They left Matudan who was to ride and fetch the other footmen from the forest, to return to Cashel with the cart of leftovers, rusted blades, and the ten remaining cows.

****

Flaithbertach lay under the black starry sky, imagining thin, flat, long blades entering his neck from different angles, to protrude the other side. He saw himself lie there, blood streaming down his neck, and tasted the hard-strong tang. He felt blades bend and dance as he played with them with his hands. Where they started, he did not know. Imaginary blades, thrust from a mind of darkness and rage, to bring the heat and blood from his throat until he felt like fire. Flaithbertach wanted to be fire. He wanted to burn and to be burned, to be an eternal fire of rage that would bring a burning heat of vengeance across this land.

"What the hell are you doing, monk?" asked Maol Muid.

Flaithbertach realized his fingers had been dancing across his throat as he lay in the dead of night, the firelight reflecting off them. He was calm. Filled with rage, but a calm, beautiful rage. "I'm an abbot, Maol Muid, not a monk. An abbot. And if you ever presume to speak to me like that again, I'll tie you to a tree and burn you alive," he liked the idea of burning someone alive. The fire attracted him, "Now go to sleep, we leave at sunrise. Or at least, don't speak to me again if you don't intend to sleep."

Maol Muid's skin tightened, as a cold breeze hit the back of his neck with Flaithbertach words. The breeze was empty. Dead somehow. Maol Muid said nothing as he watched the mad monk's fingers dance about his neck. *A strange one,* he thought. He lowered his head and slept.

The dawn came early as it was late summer. The blue gray surroundings gave little away, until the embers from the previous night's fire were reignited to shed some light. The bull had been tied to a tree, the other cows would not stray far from that great beast.

Flaithbertach, Maol Muid, and Seachnaill mounted up and rounded up the cows. A four-hour ride through the hills brought them to a thicket of bleak, skinny trees which matched the gray morning. Damp and colorless. Just like the mood of the three men. Damp and colorless. No joy. No light. Apart from the burning light in Flaithbertach's mind. He was eager for this meeting. "You're with me," he said to Seachnaill. Flaithbertach never mentioned the man's name. Seachnaill never volunteered it. He didn't want to talk to Flaithbertach if he could help it. He saw nothing holy in this monk and thought it strange that a man with such a discomforting manner could be so close to his King. Seachnaill wanted nothing more than to get back to his wife and boy, and tend his farm. Do ordinary things. Adventure was not something he craved.

Without a word, Flaithbertach was gone, cantering out of the trees, down the gray rocky hillside toward the rising smoke of a small camp. "You heard him," roared Maol Muid. "Follow him."

****

Flaithbertach was not afraid of the Norsemen. He had fought them before. Great warriors they were, but not more so than the Gaelic. These men were unlikely to attack him. They were too interested in what he offered.

He felt like he had wings, as he rode. Great wings, raised high in the air. Wings of tough, hard leather, which could not be penetrated by any sword. They pulled him high in his saddle as he approached the camp. He may have been dirty from three days on the road, but he carried himself like a King, as he drew closer the Norsemen.

The camp was at the top of a low hill, the base of which was surrounded by pointed stakes sticking from the ground at an angle, forcing any attackers to dismount and slowing them down as they approached on foot.

Flaithbertach dismounted, still feeling the great wings of leather as he stepped to the ground, his companion followed suit, as the wary eyes regarded him suspiciously.

"The priest," came a voice from the crowd, as a man stepped forward to lean against one of the wooden barriers at the base of the hill. "I am Torgny, priest. My son has told me about you. I understand you have an offer for me?"

Priest, thought Flaithbertach. He supposed that he was known as a man of God, and that is how people would see him.

"Do I look like a priest, Torgny?" Flaithbertach asked, as he walked toward the group of Norsemen. All were armed. A haphazard group carrying axes, spears, swords. Most were covered in ink and bearded, with shaved heads or long hair, or a strange mix of both. Flaithbertach recognized Canute, the gleaming jawbone still hung about his neck. He nodded in greeting.

Torgny himself was a man of a similar height to Flaithbertach, glistening white bones intertwined in his long, platted beard which came straight down from his chin. His hair was long, tied down his back, but shaved to the skin at the side to reveal the blue, gray ink tattooed on the side of his head. He was topless, showing off a broad, tattooed chest, streaked with scars. Unlike the other men, he bore no weapons.

Torgny spoke no Gaelic and Flaithbertach spoke none of the Viking languages, so they conversed in the English language of their Saxon neighbors. The Dane spoke with a strong accent, giving his words a musical quality, but he was fluent.

"Do you look like a priest? No, not really, to be honest. You look more like a killer, like me. That's good. We'll get along fine then. Come, feast with me while we talk." Flaithbertach left the bewildered Seachnaill to sit with the Vikings.

****

They sat in a dimly lit tent, a fire burning in the center. It was late morning now and Flaithbertach had not eaten. He was glad of wine, pork, and bread which was offered.

The firelight flickered, reflecting in each man's eyes, as one man took stock of the other, thinking, analyzing, and assessing what they could from outward appearances. A stranger sitting between then would perhaps, in that moment, have seen two devils look each other in the eye, each unsure whether to lash out or open their arms in friendship to a potentially powerful ally.

"What do you know of our Gods, priest?" Torgny asked in a gravelly voice.

"Your Gods," returned Flaithbertach, as he turned his gaze to his plate and pulled at a piece of pork. "What do I know of your Gods? Not much. But I would guess that you worship them, and that you pray to them. And that you make sacrifices to them," he paused to wash down his food with a gulp of wine.

Torgny smiled as Flaithbertach spoke. A polite, dangerous smile. He remained quiet and let the priest continue.

66

"I would suppose that you ask them for guidance and assistance, and act in a way that you believe would please them. I know nothing of your Gods, but based on the religion of Christ, and the old Gods of this island, and the old Gods of the Romans and the Greeks, that is what I would suppose. Is that correct, Torgny?"

"It is," replied Torgny. He smiled again and nodded, "It is, my friend. But where my Gods differ from your nailed God is how we serve. We do indeed ask for advice, and act in a way that we would suppose will please them. We do, indeed." Torgny went on, "But where we differ, my friend, is that our God does not ask us to turn the other cheek like your nailed God does. Our Gods did not die pitifully, nailed to a cross."

"I see you know something of the Christian religion," returned Flaithbertach. "Excellent. Yes, indeed," he said. "Think what you want, my friend. The nailed God is the God of a dying nation. I am taking my people back to the old ways. I am taking this island back to the old Gods. Christ is for the hapless. The Saxons across the water. The Gaelic here who will not forsake him. I am no longer a priest." He put down his food and stared at Torgny, "Those ways are dead to me. You and I will be enemies someday, of that, I have no doubt. But, for now, let us toast," he took his wine and held it up, "to a new world which you will help me build. And you will be paid handsomely in weapons and livestock."

Torgny did not raise his cup. He stared at Flaithbertach, "So, you would betray your kingdom. You would betray your religion. Why?"

"I dream of an island of old. And it starts here. In less than a year, I will be King, and at that time, if you agree to help me take the lands around me, I will help you in turn take the Saxon lands. And the Norse and the Gaelic will keep a respectful distance from one another. Help me become King and I will not forget that, even if we are on opposing sides sometime."

"What do you propose?" Torgny asked, he leaned closer. The Dane had listened quietly as Flaithbertach spoke.

"You will inspect your payment," said Flaithbertach. "If you are in agreement, you will come into my service. One of my men will remain with you," he spread his hands, "as a gesture of good faith. You will keep your payment, with the promise of more plunder and land when I become King."

"Let us not waste time then," replied the Dane.

****

Flaithbertach and Torgny arrived on horseback, with six other Norsemen, to find Maol Muid sleeping by a dying campfire, it was late evening now. The

67

Danish chief inspected the weapons and the livestock, and agreed that it was satisfactory payment for entering into Flaithbertach's service.

"We will see each other soon," Flaithbertach said, as they prepared to depart. Seachnaill remained by Torgny's side.

"One more thing," said Flaithbertach and dismounted. He approached the Viking and the Gaelic footman.

"You will have to return the cattle to your camp yourself, you have no need for a hostage now that you have been paid," he extended a hand to Seachnaill who grabbed his hand in return, glad of the fact that he would not have to return to the Viking camp.

Flaithbertach pulled him from the horse and with a strong leg, he stomped his boot into Seachnaill's face and drove the cartilage of his nose back into his brain, killing him. He stamped on the man's neck, breaking it to make certain he was dead.

"We will speak soon," Flaithbertach said and turned. "The raids can begin in five days." He walked away.

****

It was the second Sunday in March. Mass was given in the chapel at the back of the castle, followed by confession. The morning was cool and crisp, the chilled air refreshed those outside as their breath fogged around them. Men pulled cloaks tight around themselves as they shuffled toward the church. All the nobles or soldiers of rank would be there as it was expected of them.

Smoke from breakfast fires rose in a straight line through the clear, morning sky, drifting easily upward, like a gentle soul rising to the heavens.

The mad monk had returned to give council to the King. The man in black, Finnan sometimes heard him called. The black monk's robes matched Finnan's thoughts when they had first met.

It was the day after Finnan's storytelling session with the old man, the abbot had approached Finnan in the morning sun, as the dew rose in a steamy haze.

"How is your head?" he had asked, as Finnan rose from a drinking trough, after dunking his head in the freezing water, as he did every morning.

"Why do you ask?" Finnan had replied, not showing surprise at this stranger's question.

"I heard it was a late night of storytelling," replied the monk, smiling at him through a handsome blue-eyed face. The man's hair was black, but his close-cropped beard showed signs of grey.

Finnan shook his head to dry his hair. "It was," he said.

He knew the abbot was testing his reaction. What he did not know was who had told him.

He has eyes and ears everywhere, Congall had said. He hears and sees all.

Apparently, that part was true, or at least, he had eyes and ears in the common room that night.

"You will do well here," the monk said, and turned and walked away.

That was a few weeks ago, and now, the monk was back in Thomand again, attending mass in the old stone church and hearing confessions afterwards with Meonach.

Finnan was no saint. Not close to God even. He did not pray. He did not think about God. He attended mass because he respected his King's belief, but it didn't go much further than that. But now, he sat for confession with the mad monk.

"Bless me, Father, for I have sinned," he started.

"Go on, my child," came the monk's voice from the darkness like a disembodied spirit. "Tell me your sins and God will forgive you."

"My thoughts, Father," Finnan said.

There was no reply from the darkness, as Finnan waited. He could not see the other man for the windows were small and little light came through. He could just about hear Meonach's old voice drone on next door, as he administered the sacrament to other men and women of the grounds.

"My thoughts," said Finnan again. "I fear my thoughts, Father. Sometimes, I think the devil has a hold on me. I think of what I would do in defense of my King and my Queen and I see myself," he paused again. "I see myself," he continued, as he ground his teeth, "kneeling on the ground."

The monk was silent. Finnan could make out his silhouette in the darkness, as his eyes adjusted, still as a corpse, listening…silent.

Finnan let that sit a second, they were alone now; all other men had left, "I see myself kneeling on the ground…surrounded by my enemies. By the enemies of my King and Queen. They are dismembered. They are torn to pieces, much as if a pack of wild dogs had them. I see the ground slick and pooling with their blood. Their skulls are smashed, they are disemboweled, their entrails, on the ground before them. I have mutilated them, Father. I have done this to them in defense of those I serve. I dream of this. Some of them are women, youngsters, men of the cloth even." He paused again, this time for a full minute. The monk said nothing, "I have done this and I kneel in their blood. I dream of this. This is me, Father. I ask God's forgiveness. I ask God to forgive me, not for having these thoughts, but because I believe in them. These thoughts are in my dreams. They are me."

The silence hung over them like a black cloud before a storm.

"I ask God's forgiveness, Father," he said. "Grant me God's forgiveness."

The two men sat a while, then Flaithbertach spoke. "I absolve you of your sins," he said. "In the name of the Father," a cock crowed outside, "and of the son," it began to rain, "and of the holy spirit."

"Amen," both men whispered as one. And whether they knew it or not, whether they meant it or not, from that point on, regardless of either man's motives, there could be no friendship between them.

Finnan rose and left Flaithbertach in silence.

The monk was angry. His emotions were out of his control these days. He had always been quick to anger but could usually control it. He let go of the cross in his right hand which he had been squeezing so tight as to draw blood.

****

Chapter Nine

Servants and slaves buzzed in and out of the main dining area, like bees in high summer. Ten places were set under the banner of the Eoganachta, Cormac's family. The King had not entered yet, he would be the last. Anyone who entered after the King would be considered late and not welcome at the table. Cormac did not appreciate tardiness. Best to arrive before him or not arrive at all.

Two windows at the back wall let in the sun, but little light came through as it was late evening, shortly before sundown, and the day had been cloudy.

The four stone walls were lined with three torches each, the bright flames flickered, casting shadows that danced around the room, like mad demons looking for a hiding place.

A single bearskin mat lay on the floor at the front of the room, its gaping head still attached, as it stared hungrily at the table which the slaves and servants were filling with food. In front of the bearskin, a fire burned brightly. The smoke escaped to the cloudy evening through a hole in the roof. It gave the room a peaty smell. One of the slave women added wood as she passed.

Meonach was first to arrive. He was visiting Thomand and stopped at Cashel for a few days, to provide council and bring news to Cormac. He sat at a place of honor beside where Gormfhlaith would seat herself when she came in.

Wine was brought to the old priest once he arrived and he was glad to sit, for the years had taken their toll on his body. He moved slowly and sometimes with pain, and could no longer ride a horse, having traveled by cart to Cashel with a driver and a few guards. Safety was rarely an issue for him when he traveled, as the Gaelic were Christian and would not attack a priest and pagan Vikings tended to stick close to the large rivers and coast.

A few minutes later, Finnan entered. He was without his cape as it was evening and he would not be outside again. His permanent quarters were within the castle walls. He sat next to Meonach and nodded a greeting to the old priest, then demanded ale from a passing slave.

One by one, the room filled, as Ceallach, son of Ceirbeall, fostered by Cormac, entered, followed by Aodh, Cormac's other foster son, and then Matudan, Maol Muid, and Congall, all high-ranking warriors in the army of Thomand.

The conversation buzzed as ale was brought for the soldiers; Meonach stuck to his wine. Aodh's face became flushed, as he was a rake of a man, barely eighteen years old, and unusually susceptible to the potency of ale. He did his best to sit up straight and not appear drunk before his foster father; the King joined them at the table.

"You're drunk already, lad," shouted Matudan from across the table at him. He was bald as an egg and wore no beard. Rumor had it he lost a hair for every man he killed.

Aodh wore no beard either, but not because he had killed so many men, more so, because it just wouldn't grow. The small bit of ginger fluff on his chin was lost in his face, flushed as it was.

"I'm not drunk," he replied "It's just the fire. It's so damned hot in here."

"Language, my son," intoned the old priest from the other end of the table. "The heat of the fire is not so unusual that it requires a foul mouth to describe it." Meonach's education left him little patience for the misuse of the Gaelic language.

Aodh looked down, this rebuke caused him to flush even more, while Matudan roared with laughter, ignoring the serious tone of the priest.

"What news, Meonach?" called Ceallach, "I hear the Norsemen have been raiding?"

"The Norsemen are always a danger," replied Meonach. "No more this year than any other year. It is our native neighbors that worry me. The Norsemen can be reasoned with, I fear our neighbors cannot."

"To hell with reason," spat Matudan. Anger and violence were the old warrior's answer to everything. "I would march on their port to the east and burn it to the ground and every last Norseman, woman and child with them."

"My father might have a thing or two to say about a host from Munster marching though his land," Ceallach interrupted. He had little attachment to Ceirbeall Mac Muirichain, King of Leinster – his blood father, but Matudan's brash comments made him weary.

"I see," said Matudan, leaning across the table at Ceallach. "And I suppose you would ride your skinny arse like the wind and tell him that Cormac's army was marching warriors through his kingdom?"

Ceallach stared back at the old warrior as the room fell silent, apart from the sounds of the kitchen and the crackling fire. *Is he joking?* thought Ceallach.

Is he only trying to get a rise out of me or is he actually questioning my loyalty? This was a tricky one.

"No," he said. "I think I'd be too busy servicing your wife. Apparently, she needs it." He refused to look away from Matudan. He wasn't afraid of this oaf.

He held Matudan's stare for what seemed like minutes, until Matudan broke the uneasy silence with more raucous laughter. The others joined in, Maol Muid slapping Matudan's back.

The conversation resumed to the Norsemen, with Congall chiming in, eager to change the subject.

"I have fought with Norse mercenaries. Cattle raids in Connaught. Not bad men, once you are on the same side," he said, as one of the servants placed plates and warm bread around them. "Some just want a space for a farm. Decent men, the ones I fought with."

"I wouldn't mention cattle raids in front of the King, Congall," Meonach said.

"Decent men who would stab you in the back without hesitation," Maol Muid added. "Let them piss back to the frozen end of the world they came from, and plant some onions in their God-forsaken snow and ice." He helped himself to some of the bread to keep his hunger at bay.

The conversation buzzed about the room, the awkwardness gone as the ale was downed and refilled. Aodh, the King's red-headed foster son became drunker, Matudan drank more than any, without it seeming to have any effect. Maol Muid sat in conversation with Matudan, their heads close together in private discussion, Congall still spoke of Norsemen and the time he had spent with them. Everybody took Congall's words with a pinch of salt. The old warrior was notorious for embellishing stories. The old priest joined Finnan in silent contemplation, a look passed between the two men, each sensing the words earlier bore more weight than the others knew.

After a time, they had finished their bread and the great doors opened for the King and Gormfhlaith to enter and take their seats. Those gathered stood out of respect.

Cormac cut a magnificent figure as he entered the room. His white-bearded face was both noble and wise and his eyes, though tired, had a friendly, grandfatherly look. He was older than most now, and not much of a man with the sword anymore, although it did not stop him carrying one, nor did it stop him wielding the power of Thomand as a wise and prudent King.

Gormfhlaith sat first as her King pulled aside her sheepskin chair for her to sit. Cormac adored his wife and did not care if his small gestures made him seem weak or foolish.

"You may sit," he said, as he glanced to the empty seat on the right, "The abbot has not made dinner, I see." He was referring to Flaithbertach, who had been pressing for raids and incursions against the Norsemen since his monastery was attacked and his brothers massacred.

The wall hangings behind him fluttered as a gust of wind came through the back windows, there was to be more rain tonight and possibly wind. Cormac grimaced as he sat down, his guests waited until he was settled before taking their seats.

Wine was brought for the King and Queen, who thanked the slave girl kindly and addressed her by her name. All slaves were well-treated at Cashel, no matter where they came from or what their background. The King even kept a slave with skin as black as the peat bogs and teeth, white as bone. Where most people feared this man as a devil, Cormac spoke with him and treated him well and asked him about the land from which he came.

"He does not dine with you, my King?" asked Meonach.

"Flaithbertach is lost in grief," replied Cormac. "Each to their own." He looked about the men gathered, "Everybody is well? Everybody is hungry? Let us pray before we eat. Meonach, please give a blessing."

The old priest bowed his head and gave thanks to God, as the others blessed themselves.

"Do not wait for me," chimed in Cormac once the blessing was done. "Eat, my friends, eat. Aodh, what is the matter with you? Your face is flushed. Are you ill?"

This question was interrupted by a loud laugh from Matudan and Cormac understood the issue, as the bald man guffawed, "Ill tomorrow maybe," he said to even more laughter, as he drank deep from his cup of ale.

At this, men pulled legs from chickens and piled onions and carrots onto their plates and shouted for more ale as the formalities were over. Cormac pulled some beef from a wooden platter and placed it on his wife's plate.

Finnan noticed a glance pass between Matudan and Maol Muid at this, the old warrior's hairless eyebrows raising. Why would a King do the job of a slave by putting food on someone else's plate, let alone a woman's?

As the King and Queen ate with their men, they shared stories and spoke among them as equals, as wine and ale went down and a roast pig was brought from the kitchen and the chickens were devoured. The light outside faded and the wind picked up. The servants and slaves added more logs to the fire and it blazed higher.

Among the conversation and laughter, nobody noticed the abbot enter. He took a seat beside the King on his right-hand side and without a word, and began to fill his plate as Cormac noticed him.

"Ah, you join us," Cormac said, smiling, as the monk began to fill his plate.

"Yes, my King," replied Flaithbertach. He didn't look up.

"You are still sullen, my friend," the King said.

"You come to your King's table," Gormfhlaith put in "and do not excuse yourself as you walk in late?" She ignored Cormac, as he raised his forefinger to his lips, gently shushing her. "You do not ask permission to join us? You simply sit at our table and begin to eat?"

Her voice raised and some may have thought her drunk. Finnan knew different. He knew his Queen to be a fiercely loyal woman who would let no man disrespect her King and kingdom, both which she loved with all her heart. Finnan, in turn, loved Gormfhlaith because of this. He loved her and respected her and would die to protect her. He would die as quickly for his King for although he worshiped the ground Gormfhlaith walked on, he was not a jealous man and accepted that she was taken.

"My Queen," said Flaithbertach, turning his head from his plate to look her straight in the face. "I ask your pardon," he said. "My King, I ask your pardon. I will take my leave," he made to move, but Cormac pounded the table so hard with his fist that his wine tipped over and spilled on the table to drip on the ground. "Sit," he said. "Sit and be merry." Then, he laughed, "Your pardon is given but next time, it will not be. Now eat."

The meal carried on and conversation returned to normal, as bowls of apples and honey and cups of mead were brought out. The mead was sweeter than the ale and some of the men preferred it the more they drank. Laughter and loud voices echoed from the dining hall into the night, as the rain began to fall.

Chapter Ten

"Your hand," Finnan remarked, "what happened?"

"I burned my hand," Flaithbertach said, and smiled back at Finnan.

"Aye, a crucifix will do that to the devil alright."

Crucifix, Flaithbertach thought. *He couldn't know.* A figure of speech. They rode on, atop two sturdy ponies, there was a climb ahead of them.

Flaithbertach was heading back for the coast and had specifically requested from the King that Finnan accompany him.

Did he mean to kill me? Finnan thought. *He couldn't. It would be too obvious. Too much. Just because I don't trust or like this man, doesn't mean he wants to kill me. Fool!* his mind retorted. *Of course, he wants to kill you. Everyman wants to kill you. Or, at least, that is what you should believe until you have reason to think otherwise.* That was the voice of his old teacher, MacGaman, ringing in his head. The old bull, they called him. He had beaten Finnan once a week for two years, and in beating him, had hammered home every lesson he could possibly give the boy. "He wants to kill you," he would say, pointing at nobody in particular, "I want to kill you. Your brother wants to kill you."

"I don't have a brother," Finnan would reply.

Smack. A wooded staff across the face to knock him to the ground. He still had the scar.

"Everyman wants to kill you," his teacher shouted. He was beaten again. "What do we do with men who want to kill us?" MacGaman asked.

"We kill them," Finnan answered.

Smack, he was beaten with the staff again. He had that scar too, "What if you can't? You can't kill me."

"I don't know," Finnan sobbed.

The cruel, old teacher then sat down beside him in silence. "Boy," he said after a few minutes, "someday, you may be able to kill me. You pay for each lesson. You understand?" He went on, "You pay dearly and you don't deserve to, but you do. You have those scars and those memories for what you pay. But those scars and memories are what will keep you alive and what will keep your little Princess alive because she won't always be holed up in her Da's castle and all she will have is her guard."

"If you want to kill someone," he continued solemnly, "you watch them. You learn. You listen. You wait. You move. Move the pieces and set it up for a time when you are strong enough." He paused as if he thought of something and looked down at the youth, "You ever play chess, Finnan?"

"No," Finnan replied, bracing himself for another smack. It didn't come.

"You should learn," he said. "I will teach you. Those lessons will be free. No violence. Now, up. Grab your sword."

And so, during the day, MacGaman would teach Finnan the ways of the warrior after he had learned his languages, philosophy, and religion, and he would beat him on occasion, although it became less and less frequent as Finnan grew into his late teenage years, and became a strong and confident fighter.

"The time is coming," MacGaman said over a game of chess, one night late into the evening darkness, "when you will be able to kill me. I don't blame you if take the chance. I have been a cruel teacher, but you are the better of it."

He had been a cruel teacher, but Finnan was the better of it. He did not kill MacGaman. Perhaps one day, but not yet.

Finnan and Flaithbertach rode on in silence, the evening sun at their backs. Finnan had instructed Ceallach to follow him. Cormac's foster son had listened to Finnan's misgivings about the dark monk. He was not convinced, but both men trusted each other. Ceallach agreed to follow them at a distance. "You don't trust me," said the monk.

"What does it matter?" Finnan asked, he didn't look at him.

"It matters," Flaithbertach said. "Not to me, but to your King. He trusts me. I have advised him for years, you know."

"I know."

"But you don't trust me."

"No, I don't," Finnan said. "Nor you me."

Flaithbertach looked back at him, the light caught the scar on his face. There was always something in the monk's eyes when he looked at you. He guided his pony through the heather of the low-lying mountains, darkness was close. "I don't like you, Finnan. One word to Cormac and I could have you gone. He listens to me, you know."

"Could you," Finnan replied dryly. "At least we understand each other. Why don't you be rid of me then, or is that why you brought me out here?"

"Ha-ha," Flaithbertach laughed out loud, throwing his head back, mouth open wide. "Oh, I wouldn't be so predictable. Besides, maybe this little trip will help us settle our differences. What is it you don't like about me?"

"Why doesn't a shepherd like a wolf?" Finnan asked.

"Because they're afraid of wolves," Flaithbertach answered. "Because they're afraid. Are you afraid, Finnan?"

"I've killed many a wolf in my day, my friend, and I've never lost a sheep."

They rode on in silence for a while. It would be shortly time to make camp. The fire would let Ceallach know their position. Finnan would keep the fire burning high, as long as all was well.

"Yes. Strange that the only thing keeping you at Thomand now is your sheep."

"My sheep?" Finnan asked.

"Your Queen."

"Careful, wolf," said Finnan. "I would waste no time spilling your blood if you speak ill of the Queen."

"There will be no blood spilled tonight, calm yourself." It was obvious to Flaithbertach now. It had been too easy. He had found Finnan's weakness in the lost sheep. The Leinster Princess, pretending to be Queen of Munster. *But for how long,* he thought, as he dismounted, sighing, "I think we have spoken enough, Finnan. Share my fire and food or be gone. It is up to you, but I am done arguing."

He has what he needs, Finnan thought, disgusted with himself. He had let his emotions get the better of him.

****

Ceallach listened in the darkness, but heard nothing, save the howl of a lone wolf or dog off in the distance. The sun had gone down behind the mountains in the west and darkness was descending quickly.

He knew Finnan would camp in the open, so he had chosen his watch point accordingly. He had no idea why he was out here, freezing his bollocks off to watch Finnan's fire from the distance. Finnan and Flaithbertach were probably having a huge laugh about him.

"No fires," Finnan had told him. "Yes, yes, I know," Ceallach agreed, but he would risk a small one when it was full dark and shelter it with some rocks. It was not unusual for another traveler to be camping out here in the middle of the night.

He and Finnan were becoming good friends. He trusted him and saw Finnan's devotion to his foster father and foster mother. "The dark monk is unusual, Finnan, I agree," Ceallach had said. "A madman even, but he's trusted here. Why do you doubt him?"

It was the look in Finnan's eyes that convinced him, His friend was worried, truly worried about something. "Just do this for me, Ceallach," Finnan had said to him. Whatever Finnan was doing, he only had good intentions.

Flaithbertach was a strange one, he thought, pulling his woolen cloak tight around him, he threw his sword belt to the ground before him as he started to build a small rock wall to shelter the meager fire he would build. A strange one indeed, but he had been his foster father's friend and advisor for many years. One of the King's closest advisors, in fact. He could not believe Flaithbertach would have anything but the King and kingdom's best interests at heart.

Here he was, regardless, watching Finnan's back, as Finnan headed into the sticks with the monk, accompanying him part way back to the coast. Flaithbertach could take care of himself, Ceallach knew, it was strange that he requested Finnan accompany him.

The fire down below burned in the distance, its warm glow enticed him. He could hear faint voices carry on the soft breeze, but could not make out any words and they soon fell silent as the black of night engulfed him.

Although there was a full moon two nights ago, it had since clouded over, and he was surrounded by a heavy darkness. There would be a noticeable glow from his fire, but he didn't care. He wasn't sitting here in the cold, pitch black.

His foster brother, Aodh, trusted Flaithbertach, he thought to himself, as he set some kindling together under a triangle of small twigs and struck his flint. Aodh was young and at times, foolish, and he trusted everybody. Aodh thought the only enemies were outside of the kingdom. He was astounded to find the King's cattle had been stolen by thieves within their own kingdom.

Ceallach sat in silent contemplation throughout the night. All this talk from Finnan had made him uneasy. He dozed some, but remained in a seated position so he would not fall into a deep slumber, and the fire below burned all night until the first pink rays of dawn light reached into the sky from the east.

****

Finnan was up at sunrise. He added more sticks to the fire, it was little use as a signal now, but the morning was cold and he could see his breath.

"Was that your man up on the hill last night?" Flaithbertach asked.

Finnan couldn't blame Ceallach for lighting a fire.

"I had no man on the hill," he said. "I will take my leave now."

"I wouldn't blame you, although I think if we were to fight, it would be tough to choose a victor."

A compliment, thought Finnan. Flaithbertach was indeed strange, but no doubt his words of praise were designed to throw him off.

He walked over to the nearby stream without reply and ducked his face in the ice-cold, flowing water and held it there for a few moments. Flaithbertach watched him as he rose and stretched.

"How did you sleep?" he asked Finnan.

"Soundly."

"Soundly? I lost count of how many times you were up to keep the fire going."

"It was cold," Finnan said. Flaithbertach missed nothing, even in his sleep. "I didn't see you get up. You would have let us freeze, would you?"

"I wasn't cold," Flaithbertach said, waving his hand, he walked to his pony to throw on the saddle. "Keep safe, Finnan, it is no harm you have a friend up there in the hills, there are bandits and Norsemen about, according to reports. Until next time."

Neither man offered a handshake and the monk rode off without looking back.

Finnan saddled up and headed in the direction he had seen Ceallach's fire last night. They would not be safe until they were back within the walls of Thomand.

****

"Keep alert," Finnan said to Ceallach when they rejoined.

"You expect trouble?" the younger man asked.

"Always, especially out here, just the two of us."

"How did that go last night?" Ceallach asked. "Did you kiss?" he teased.

"Ceallach, for fuck's sake, do I look like I'm in the mood for jokes?" Finnan complained.

"Well, I froze my arse here all night for you, so I am in the mood for jokes. And I could do with a short snooze before we head out. I haven't slept."

"Alright then, I'm sorry," said Finnan. He felt bad for his harshness. Ceallach had agreed to watch him from a distance without a word of complaint. "A short one then. I'll fix a bit of breakfast, I have some pheasant."

And a short snooze it was, Ceallach swore by the short snoozes, the man could sleep anywhere and would be fresh after. Finnan marveled at this, seeing it almost as a gift from God.

They set out after a quick breakfast and threw dirt over the fire before riding away, down the rocky slopes until they came to an open valley below.

A trail cut through the thick, purple heather which spread out in all directions. *A perfect place for an ambush,* Finnan thought, there could be fifty men hiding in the heather and they would not be seen, he circled around and drew his sword. His spine twitched and stomach was uneasy. "If it can happen, it will happen," he said.

MacGaman had told him that. "Maybe not now," he had said from across the chessboard, "but some time." If there could be men in the heather, there would be men in the heather. Maybe not on this occasion, but on some occasion.

"What are you muttering?" Ceallach asked. "You're giving me nerves."

****

"You should have nerves. I told you. We're not safe. I don't trust that bastard black monk."

"He's no—"

"I don't want to hear it," Finnan cut him off. "I told you, I don't trust him and that's the end of it. Now is not the time to debate this."

Both men turned about on their horses and surveyed the surrounding landscape, listening. There was no sound, save the crows and a sheep or a goat in the distance.

"Nothing," said Ceallach.

"Nothing…that we can see," Finnan said, staring hard at the heather which surrounded them each side of the trail.

He dismounted and walked off the dirt, horse-trodden trail into the bush, slowly, as if he were walking into a pit of snakes, or something worse. Some unseen blackness that would swallow him up.

"What is it?" Ceallach hissed. He was silenced by a swift wave of the other man's hand.

"Ceallach, I think—"

"Smoke," Ceallach interrupted.

"Yes, there's a farm nearby. I have stopped there many times," replied Finnan.

"No, too much smoke. Look."

Indeed, there was a pillar of black smoke rising off to the east, dark against the white clouds. "God help us, the farm must be burning. Let us go, Ceallach."

Finnan had seen movement, in the heather, out of the corner of his eye, but they could not delay.

They arrived to a cluster of small buildings. A wattle house with a thatched roof and two smaller sheds. The sheds were bright with flame and there were dead animals on the ground when the riders skidded to a halt to assess the scene.

The animals had been disemboweled; their innards left trailing about the small open area by the sheds. Two cows, a goat, and a dog. Disemboweled and beheaded, blood still dripped from them and pooled on the ground below. The heads of the cows had been mounted on stakes, protruding from the ground, like ominous sentries from hell, the dog's head lay on the ground beside them.

The two men dismounted. "This blood is fresh. This just happened," said Ceallach.

"Look for tracks, I'll see what's left of them."

"What's left of them?"

"Just look for tracks," Finnan replied and headed for the house. The fire was starting to recede now as there wasn't much in the meager buildings to burn. The house had been left untouched for a reason, he thought, as he stepped through the doorway into the gloom.

Finnan was a hard man. A warrior. He had killed many men, but he was not a butcher of families and what he saw brought anger and disgust in equal measure.

A figure sat at a small table, propped into a sitting position with a sharp long branch driven into his back. He could tell from the blood-stained clothes it was a man. His head had been removed and in its place sat the head of the decapitated goat from the farmyard. It was held in place with another sharp, well-chosen branch, one end jammed into the stump between the man's shoulders, the other jammed up into the goat's head. The devil eyes stared back at him.

A child hung by the neck from the ceiling, slowly revolving in a gentle circle in a final sad dance.

"Jesus," said Ceallach from behind him. "Jesus, who did this?"

Finnan's eyes hurt from the smoke and from the scene of dread in front of him.

"I need air," he said. "We'll bury these people and be on our way."

"There were tracks. Ten or twelve men maybe. Headed back the way we came."

"They were in the bush. They were in the shitting, God-forsaken bush. They'll be well ahead now. Those shit-filled bastards. Devils. Shit-ridden, rotting devils," he bent over and retched, vomiting up the half-digested remains of the pheasant breakfast they had shared.

"Shit," Ceallach said in a whisper. "Cunts. What do we do? Do we follow?"

"We bury these people and get away from this evil deed. Two of us chasing them won't achieve anything," Finnan said, and wiped the stinking vomit from his chin.

Ceallach was white like a ghost. He fell to his rump and sat. "Yes," he said after a few moments. "Yes, we'll bury them."

****

The two men removed the heads from the spikes and buried the bodies. The priest could return later to give them a proper send off. It was near dark by the time they had finished, so they set camp for the night on high ground close by and took turns to keep watch for the return of whatever enemy had desecrated these innocents.

The return trip to Thomand passed without further incident, Finnan was lost in thought as he brought his horse through the old wooden gates and dismounted. "Have her cleaned and fed, and have a fresh mount ready to go by midday," he told a servant boy.

"We best see the King," said Ceallach.

"We best." Finnan's expression was not lost on the soldiers, servants, and tradesmen around him, as he walked up the path toward the castle. Rumor always spread fast, even if there was nothing to tell. Unfortunately, this time, there was news to talk of and much to speculate on.

"Who do you think it was?" Cormac asked Finnan. The aging King sat at a writing desk, quill in hand, marking some parchment before him, his priest, Meonach, sat beside him in silent thought. Each man held a cup of wine. Also present were Ceallach, Matudan, and Aodh, the fresh-faced redhead. He looked worried.

"Norsemen, southerners, Connaught men…who knows. I saw no sign of them. I felt them, but saw no sign. I find it hard to believe though, that Christians would carry out such acts as these."

"Norsemen, yes," boomed Matudan in his commanding voice. "Perhaps." Matudan was not one for wine, preferring to swig ale to help him contemplate these issues. He drained his cup, "Or Leinstermen, my King. Norsemen will not likely stray so far from their ships and their rivers. More likely the Leinstermen, I say."

"This is the third raid in as many weeks," Meonach chimed in. "My King, we need a show of strength, even if it is not the Leinstermen, we need a show of strength."

The King put down his quill and drummed his fingers on the table, "Flaithbertach. When did you leave him?"

"Yesterday morning, my King."

"Aodh, quickly now, make ready. You may catch him before he reaches the water and sets sail. I want him back here with haste. Take five men. If you don't reach him by nightfall tomorrow, send a messenger and return to me."

"You think we need him, my King?" the question from Finnan raised a hairless eyebrow from Matudan, and Ceallach gave him a look to silence him, but the King did not react.

"Yes," he replied. "Aodh, leave now. Matudan, ready your men."

The old warrior left at once without a word.

"Ceallach, you and Finnan will take five men with Meonach, to grant those poor people peace. Now, leave me," said the King.

His foster sons filed out, followed by Meonach and Finnan.

"Finnan, please remain."

"My King?" Finnan asked.

"You have reason to think the abbot is not required?" Cormac inquired.

"I have no reason, my King," replied Finnan.

"Then why do you ask?" Cormac pressed.

"Well, is he of use to us?" replied Finnan. "Do you trust him?"

"Careful, Finnan. Not from me, but Flaithbertach is a powerful man, and yes, I do trust him. You do not want him as an enemy. He is quick to anger and ruthless, but his council here is valued." Cormac sat back and rested his weary head in his hands, "I do not want bad blood in my chambers, especially between my most trusted advisors."

Finnan's mouth twitched. "There is no bad blood," he said.

"No?" Cormac looked up. His pale-blue eyes, tired, "Then why do you doubt him? I see it in you. I see your unease."

Little could be hidden from him. Only the most cunning of enemies could sneak one past this man. And Flaithbertach was most cunning, Finnan thought.

"I don't know, my Lord. He bothers me. He isn't one of us, my King. He…" Finnan struggled to find the words, scratching at his stubbled face. "I can't put my finger on it. He is damaged. His mind is torn."

"How do you see this?" Cormac inquired.

"I don't know," answered the warrior. "I just do."

"Yes, his mind is torn." He paused, "It is. But I do trust him, Finnan." He stood and folded the paper he had been working on. "I do," he said, this time to himself.

"Will that be all?" Finnan asked, eager to get the grisly task over with.

"It will." Cormac watched Finnan leave. A tall sturdy warrior, who had an eye for his young wife, he knew, but Cormac trusted Finnan. More so because of the love this man bore for Cormac's wife. It had been obvious to him from the beginning. Maybe Finnan did not realize it himself, Cormac thought. He had never overstepped his boundaries and he had proven himself again and again. He was a warrior of unbounded loyalty.

"I hope you are wrong, young man," he whispered, as he sat back down.

****

Flaithbertach arrived back at the Halls of Thomand in four days, accompanied by Aodh and the other riders. He sat in council for many hours that day, alone with Cormac.

"What are our options?" Flaithbertach asked, eying Cormac through his dark eyes, his black beard was beginning to turn grey. It framed a serious face.

"To fight," replied the King. "I see no other way. It will lead to that. It always does," he continued and stood to pace in front of the great stone fireplace in his private council room. The fire was blazing, although it was summer time, it was cold outside. "I have already called my banners. The armies are gathering. What will we do? We will talk and then what will happen?" Cormac was uncertain. He did not want to fight, but the raids from the Leinstermen showed him they wanted it. Even if the attacks were not carried out by Leinster, the weapons and armor they had sent in tribute was clearly intended to be an insult.

"I cannot appear weak, Flaithbertach. I do not want to be the aggressor here, but we must make a show of force."

"They are the aggressors. They have already attacked," Flaithbertach replied. "You are not the aggressor for defending your land."

"What sort of King am I, if I drag us into a war? The best case is that we ravage each other and the farmers, fishermen, and ordinary people suffer and die. It could be years of fighting and famine, for all I know. Years. A war with Leinster could destroy us."

He sat back down and buried his face in his hands. *Beware the serpent who falls...* he remembered the pale-faced man's words. *The serpent who falls. Ceirbeall? The Norsemen?*

"What of Flan Sinna?" asked the monk, interrupting his thoughts. "Will he help?"

"I cannot reach him without crossing Ceirbeall's territory."

"What of your new friends?" Flaithbertach asked.

"The Norsemen are of no use to me. I cannot ask for peace with them and then, my first request is for them to join me in battle. Why will they help me anyway?"

Flaithbertach stood and crossed the stone floor to the table. He cut himself a piece of bread and chewed thoughtfully. His feet were bare, the flagstone cold on his soles, he sat again, closer to the fire, to warm them.

"I will go to them," he said with an air of finality, as if the solution was already there, staring them in the face.

"Go to them and do what?" asked Cormac.

"I will go to them and treat with Ceirbeall. I will tell him we want peace, but these incursions cannot be accepted. I will tell him we want compensation and in return, we can become neighbors in peace and trade. I will go to him first light. Let us prepare."

Cormac nodded, "It is worth a try, my friend. Take my sons with you. Now, let us now pray."

Chapter Eleven

It was midmorning when the three riders crested the hill to get their first glimpse of the great halls of Ceirbeall Mac Muirichain, King of Leinster. Smoke rose from the settlement in the distance, the fortress further back on the crest of the next hill was maybe an hour's ride away.

Aodh and Ceallach were nervous for different reasons. Although Aodh had killed men in battle, he was young and he had never rode into a lion's den before, with so little protection. Ceallach was silent for different reasons, he had no wish to be here in the first place. These halls were a thing of the past for him, at least until Ceirbeall, his blood father, died.

They were accompanied by ten riders from Cormac's personal guard. Although they were expected, the foster sons of the King of Thomand would not travel through hostile territory unguarded. Matudan had not accompanied them, he had other matters to attend to after the horrors at the farm. Matudan and Ceallach parted ways in the courtyard with a handshake, "Enjoy the reunion with your father," the shiny-headed warrior had said and then pulled the younger man closer, whispering in his ear, "Maybe he'll teach you some manners."

They rode on in silence, Flaithbertach lead the way. Aodh and Ceallach were fast friends, but the mad monk's heavy presence weighed down on them and did not make for much conversation.

They pressed on, descending the hills through a thicket of young trees, swaying blissfully in the cool breeze. The sun was shining now, though their clothes were wet after morning rain. The two foster brothers hoped they would be treated as guests and allowed a meal and a bath, regardless of the discussions.

The group rode on and picked up speed as they rode past the round wooden buildings, with thatched roofs, which littered the countryside here and there, as they grew nearer to the fortress. The banner of Cormac Mac Cuileneann was held high for all those to see, though no peasant farmers would risk attacking a group of armed men on horseback.

"Ceallach," called Flaithbertach over his shoulder, as the horses slowed to a trot to make their way up the narrow track, ascending the hill to the fortress gates. They were minutes away now and could make out the wooden walls and the pointed stakes protruding menacingly, like jagged teeth waiting to impale them.

"I want you to wait with the men. We don't want to be upsetting your father by bringing you to him, making demands on behalf of Cormac."

"What makes you think he would be upset by me?" Ceallach replied, as he checked his surroundings. He had known these lands as a boy until the age of twelve, before he was brought away. In truth, he was glad not to have to face his father. At least, not until after words had been exchanged.

The men dismounted to the sound of a horn blowing at the gates, signaling their arrival.

"With me, Aodh," said Flaithbertach sharply. "Ceallach, hold off with the men until you are called."

The men were met by Diarmuid, son of Ceirbeall and blood brother to Ceallach, when the gates opened. The two brothers did not look at each other, as Diarmuid addressed Flaithbertach, "You and your men would eat?"

"I will not eat. Aodh and I will see the King as soon as he is able. Your brother and the soldiers can eat if you have a place prepared."

"The King is ready," replied Diarmuid, as the gate closed behind them. "Let our men see to your horses. Follow me," he said and turned to walk through the grounds toward the main building.

Aodh followed behind Flaithbertach and tried not to look nervous, as he took note of the soldiers' positions. They walked the ramparts atop the walls, up and down, with a good vantage point over the men below. Each man carried a spear and a sword at his side. More men littered the lower levels. All watched the newcomers, all were armed.

The doors to the great hall opened and the men stepped into the gloom, led by Diarmuid. They walked up a long hall, again lined with soldiers who watched silently. The doors closed behind them, blocked out what little daylight had come through, as they approached a raised platform where Ceirbeall, the King of Leinster, sat to receive them.

"Why have you come?" his flat voice echoed. His face was blank and uninterested. He was a tall, muscular man, with hair cut short, and a black bushy beard. His heavily tattooed forearms held a sword across his lap as he stared at them.

A show of bravado, thought Flaithbertach. He did not care. He was not impressed by men who sat in chairs making demands. Actions were what impressed Flaithbertach. Actions were what demonstrated power, not beautiful, unused blades sitting on a King's lap.

"King Ceirbeall," began Flaithbertach formally. "Thanks to you for receiving us, and thank you for the offer of hospitality. Our men are tired as you can imagine."

"I don't give a shit for your manners or your men. What do you want of me? Time is precious, Flaithbertach. I make an offering to your King and then my borders are raided. Explain this, before I have you disemboweled and send your head back to your King."

"Very well," replied Flaithbertach. Aodh marveled at the monk's composure as the monk went on, "Yes, your borders have been raided." This surprised Aodh. His foster father had made no raids on Leinster. There had been some raids in Munster's territory, but Cormac had held off on retaliation as he had been advised by Flaithbertach to send emissaries to sit and break bread with the King of Leinster. A task he and his foster brother had been put forward for. What raids was Ceirbeall talking about? And why was Flaithbertach agreeing with this?

"My King was not satisfied with the offering you made, so he sent men into Leinster to make things right. He is now more satisfied having taken what he believes to have been rightfully owed to him and sends his foster sons to you to demand an end to this and resume peaceful relations."

"He demands," spat Ceirbeall. "Your King makes demands of me? I send him cattle and arms, he raids my territories and he comes to me with demands?" *Cattle and arms,* thought Aodh. Arms came in homage. Rusted old arms that the poorest mercenary would not wear, let alone a King's soldier, but no cattle arrived at Thomand.

He made to speak but was cut off by Ceirbeall, who rose to his feet, the sword on his lap clattering to the stone floor below, echoing through the room, the sound drowned out by the King's voice, "Explain this, monk. And where is my son. Was that little shit afraid to come to me with this news?" He bent to pick up the fallen sword and took a step down toward the men, as he shook with rage, the soldiers around him tensed as they stood at the ready.

"Your son declined to enter, he preferred to dine with the soldiers," Flaithbertach replied. He did not flinch at the King's tone.

This last discrepancy was too much for Aodh and he managed to blurt out, "My lord…" he said in a flustered stutter, but he was unable find the words. "My lord…" he stammered again, his face became redder, his skin burned, he had forgotten why he was even here now. Flaithbertach was supposed to do all the talking. He was only there to show Cormac's commitment to peace, but now, Flaithbertach was speaking of cattle raids carried out by Thomand.

Ceirbeall stood and stared at Aodh as if he had just noticed him. The sword hung from his right hand.

"You wish to continue, Aodh?" Flaithbertach asked. He waited another moment and addressed Ceirbeall again. "My Lord, we come to you with an end to this situation," he said, as he unfastened his battle axe from his side. He was not within striking distance of the King, however, the soldiers were in front of him in a flash, an iron-tipped spear held to Flaithbertach's face. Although Ceirbeall appreciated his men's wits, he motioned them to stand down, he was curious now as Flaithbertach held the axe across the palms of his hands.

"If you will, my Lord, allow me to prove my intentions."

Aodh watched Flaithbertach in disbelief. Flaithbertach was about to swear allegiance to Ceirbeall. "No!" he said. "No, Flaithbertach, what are you doing?" he had finally found his tongue.

Ceirbeall watched as the red-haired man shouted in anguish at his companion. It would take more than the axe of the King of Thomand's closest advisor to change his opinion on matters.

"Aodh," the monk flashed him a look, "be still, this is all in order." He turned his attention back to Ceirbeall, "Bear with me, good King, I am coming to the point of this business." He stooped to a squat, deliberately not kneeling, Ceirbeall noted. "You remember what you asked me before?"

What is he doing? Aodh thought, as he watched Flaithbertach remove the leather glove from his left hand and place his palm on the cold stone slabs, fingers spread. He took the large axe in his right hand and held the blade to the knuckle of his left forefinger and pushed it through, severing the finger, warm blood flowed across the flagstones. The pain was blinding, Flaithbertach gritted his teeth.

"This, you can use," he said. He turned to Aodh and with a sudden ferocity, he thrust the butt of the axe into the boy's face and knocked the young man to the ground. Ceirbeall made an automatic jump forward in surprise.

Aodh's nose stung as the warm blood gushed down his face. The pain was not so bad yet, but he knew it was coming, the bones in his nose were shattered. He fell to his rump on the stone floor and put his hands to his face. He looked up at Flaithbertach, his friend. The monk put a foot to Aodh's chest and pressed him into the ground. He found it hard to breathe as he tried to push up. Flaithbertach pushed down with his boot. "Sssssshhh," the monk said, and released his foot. The last thing Aodh saw was the mad monk's blade coming down on his chest, smashing cleanly through his ribs, into his heart, as Flaithbertach brought his axe down with one blow, killing the foster son of his King and closest friend.

"My Lord, please forgive me for spilling blood in your halls," Flaithbertach said, as he stepped away from his dead companion and bent to pick up his finger. "But I fear it was necessary to convince you of my intentions. This will help," he said, as he tossed the finger at Ceirbeall's feet and wound a rag around his hand, the pain becoming unbearable, "I need you to tend to my hand."

Ceirbeall looked down at the bloodied digit on the floor in front of him and the broken body. It was split open down the middle of his chest, from the bottom of his neck down to the abdomen, the dark blood flowed over the flag stones.

"Have someone clean this mess up," he shouted, "and get someone in to tend this wound. I'm listening." he said to Flaithbertach. He had never seen such disrespect, nobody spilled blood in this room but him, but the mad monk had his attention.

****

Ceallach entered his father's great hall, accompanied by two of his soldiers either side of him. Flaithbertach and his foster brother were nowhere to be seen. A slave girl was on her hands and knees before the throne, scrubbing the ground.

"Father," he called when he reached the throne.

"Silence," replied Ceirbeall to his son. "You do not address me until I give you leave to."

He stepped down from his throne and stood before his son. They looked at each other, anger hung in the air between both men. Suddenly, Ceirbeall brought his head forward with force and butted his son in the forehead, flooring him. As Ceallach fell, his two guards were speared from behind and cast to one side before they were finished off with a spear to the chest. Their bodies were carried off as Ceallach was picked up and punched hard in the stomach by his father.

"Your foster brother is dead," Ceirbeall said. "Your monk is in my dungeon. This finger bears his ring if you doubt me. You will take it to your foster father and explain to him that I am marching on Thomand. He will submit to me or his monk will die and we will meet in the battlefield. You can stay with me, Ceallach. Stay and redeem yourself."

Ceallach could not reply as he gasped for breath. He knew his two guards were dead. He could hear the commotion outside as the rest of his men were butchered. He tried to stand up straight, but still could not catch his breath. He shook his head. "Redeem myself?" he spluttered. "For what?"

Ceirbeall shook his head and said, "If you have to ask, there is no point in us talking." He looked down at his son, gasping for air on his hands and knees. "You are my son," he said. "I will not kill you. Stay or go, what will it be?"

Ceallach spat, "I would rather die than serve you." He got to his knees and stood. He still gasped as his father grabbed his hair and pulled his head back. Ceirbeall brought the tip of his knifepoint to Ceallach's eyebrow and dug the knife point in hard, as he dragged it down through the eyeball, slicing through it in a spray of blood and thick sticky liquid. His son screamed in pain and grief as the reality of what was happening sunk in to him.

His men were dead, his foster brother murdered by his own blood father. His face was a mass of pain as he was carried outside and thrown on a horse which carried him out the wooden gates he had entered just hours before. He had nowhere to go but home, to carry his father's message of war to his adopted kingdom.

****

Ceallach's horse plodded along at a slow pace, its rider inconsolable. Summer flies buzzed about his head, attracted by the warm blood and puss which dripped from his eye. It was strange to Ceallach, to be in such agony and to hear the birds singing sweetly around him. His eye burned with a great pain and a horrible itch inside of the socket, it had been sliced apart by his father's blade. He knew he would die if he did not get help quickly. He did not care. He was slumped forward on his horse, a lifeless figure tracking across the horizon, allowing the animal to go where it would.

There was immense physical pain, but it was the pain in his mind which hurt the most. The pain of grief. He had just lost his father in the worst way imaginable, when Ceirbeall put that knife to his eye. There was no going back. They were both dead to each other. Ceirbeall had chosen this course of action, Ceallach had not, but he was the one who suffered for it now. He was alone now. His one remaining eye wept the tortured tears of a desperate man as the blood flowed from his damaged face.

He still felt the cold blade cutting through his eyebrow and into the softness in his eye socket, as he watched his father drag the blade down his face.

He saw his mother walk alongside him as delirium took hold, she did not speak. He tried to lift his arm but felt weak, as fever took charge of his body. She simply looked back, her face sad. Was she sad for him? he wondered, Would she mourn him? "Maybe he'll teach you some manners," he heard a voice whisper. Who was it that had said that? He faded into unconsciousness as a rider approached from behind.

****

It was evening time in Thomand, church bells tolled as the sun sank. The rain had abated and the sky was clear, as a rider was spotted from the castle gates. Flaithbertach's Vikings, led by the Norseman, Torgny, had found Ceallach, wandering aimless.

"He may die, my King," Meonach, the old priest, had told Cormac. "He may die, he may live."

"They are all gone, Meonach," Cormac whispered. "They are all gone, I sent them."

Meonach turned and took the King by the shoulders, "We don't know. Flaithbertach is alive, that is for sure. They are keeping him alive."

"Then why send me his finger?"

"Proof, Cormac," Meonach said. "Proof, otherwise it is useless. Come, let us leave Ceallach to rest."

They turned out to the corridor and walked through the shadowy torchlight toward his private chapel. The two old men shuffled along. They may as well have been lame beggars, rather than a King of men and advisor to the powerful.

The door in front of them opened suddenly, as Finnan hurried in, "How is he?"

"He may live," Cormac replied.

"Flaithbertach is alive," Finnan said.

"I hope so," Cormac said, "Come, let us pray."

"No," Finnan said, "He is alive. He is here."

"How?" Cormac's eyes narrowed. "How is he here?"

"How indeed," Finnan repeated. "He needs attending, Meonach, will you come?"

Chapter Twelve

"We must fight them," Flaithbertach raged. "We must fight them, my King."

"Flaithbertach," Cormac countered. The old sage sat back wearily in his chair and placed his leathery hands over his wrinkled face.

"If you can't, then I will," Flaithbertach shouted, as he rose to his feet. "I will," he roared. "I will avenge your son."

"My son, Flaithbertach," Cormac shouted back and thumped his chest. "I know my loss, I know the pain. My son is dead and another maimed."

"And what will you do? Your son, yes, but my friend, I know this loss too, Cormac, I feel this loss. My friend," he shouted, "and my brothers burned alive. I am lucky to be here. Why am I here, Cormac? Why was I spared?"

Cormac lifted his head and looked at his old friend. Flaithbertach was not the same. He never would be. Especially not now. Not after this. "You were lucky, Flaithbertach. Luck."

"Twice, Cormac. I was spared twice. By God." Flaithbertach rose and threw his goblet of wine against the wall, "God has given us a chance to avenge your son and my brothers, and you talk about luck?"

"Do not forget yourself, Flaithbertach," Cormac warned. "I find myself repeating this to you of recent times."

"I do not forget myself, my King," Flaithbertach dropped to his knees before Cormac. They were in his private chambers. Cormac had shrunk into himself as if with the loss of his son he had lost some of himself too. "I do this for you," Flaithbertach continued. "I make the argument you do not want to hear." He took the King's hand in his, "I speak roughly but from a gentle heart. A gentle heart that bleeds, Cormac. I have lost so much."

He stood and walked to the door and turned, "They are coming, my King, make no mistake, they are coming. Let us bring the fight to them or this kingdom will burn. Ride out or no, but the fight is coming." He left, the black monk's words rang in Cormac's ear. "The fight is coming," he said to himself. He was too old and weary to fight and his son was dead.

He sat in silence for a time, until the shadows grew long in the room. The sun was setting outside of his window, a crow called as it passed his chamber.

Did it mock him? Was it a warning? *Beware the serpent who falls,* he thought to himself. "Just a crow," he muttered. "A bird, you old fool."

He stood and paused as his back ached. "Desmond," he called. "Get the fire going, will you," he asked when his servant entered. "The fight is coming," he muttered, remembering Flaithbertach's words. The servant turned at this, "No, Desmond, I am speaking to myself." He sat again and poured himself a cup of water. The water was cold for the castle was cold, he believed in the power of water. Holy water, yes, but the refreshing power of drinking water cleansed the body and mind. *Everything in moderation,* he thought – apart from water. Everything else.

The fire was going now, as the room darkened with the setting sun and Desmond went to leave.

"A fire," his wife said, as she entered the room. "Desmond, you may go. Thank you for the fire. He would freeze, you know," she said, as the servant left the room.

"And wasn't it I who asked him to light it?" Cormac replied.

"A wonder," she said, putting her hand on his shoulder. "You argued with the monk."

"You heard?"

"Cormac, I'm next door."

"And?"

"And what?" she asked, pulling a chair up to the table he sat at. She saw the age in his face, the last year had been hard on him.

"The fight is coming, whether we ride out or not, Gormfhlaith."

"I heard the monk's words," she said, as she picked wax from the candle on the table. She held it to the flame to melt it.

"You do not trust him?" he asked.

"I do not. Do you?"

"I do," he said. "He is my oldest friend. He may be antagonistic and argumentative, but his council is sound, Gormfhlaith. The fight is coming."

"What will you do then?" her voice was far away, as she gazed at the burning candle. It was as if she spoke to herself.

"The only thing I can do," Cormac rose and walked to the fire and crouched before it. He held his hand outstretched, "You have served me, my Queen."

"Served you? I love you."

"You do, I know, but you did not choose me, you did your part for peace and you served me as a wife and a Queen, and gave me more than I ever asked for. I owe you."

"You owe me? You owe me nothing," she told him.

"I owe you, my love, I owe Desmond, I owe the farmers in those fields, and I owe the people here. I must keep the fight from you all." He stood, "We will ride out, and soon. I have wasted too much time."

She admired him. She saw the great strength in him to do the things he did not want to do. The strength to ride to battle when he was fit only for a quiet life in his twilight years. The strength to ride out to keep those he loved safe. Those he served.

"Rest, my King. Preparations will start tomorrow. You rest and I will inform Finnan of your decision."

"Thank you," he would forget about it until morning. Or, at least try to. Silent contemplation would ease his mind.

Gormfhlaith turned to leave, but something came to mind and she paused. "Beware, my King," she said. "Beware of that black monk. I do not like him."

****

Within two days, the banner men of Munster were gathered and ready to ride, and a long column stretched from Thomand like a great broken snake, sprawled across the land under a grey sky. The warriors were there to fight, supported by their servants, cooks, priests, carts of food, and supplies. Tradesmen came along, the odd merchant. Some mercenaries, among them Flaithbertach's Norsemen, were scattered here and there. Whores tagged along near the end, the King did not like their way of life, though he would condemn nobody for trying to make a living by whatever means necessary.

The journey brought them east across his kingdom, as they snaked through the valley between the mountains, the King traveled in a cart covered in canvas, he slept for much of the time.

Ceallach had recovered from his injuries enough to be able to ride again, and had trained with a sword, though he rode alone for most of the journey. Finnan had tried to speak to his friend, but he was lost to the world in a murky sea of confusion and hatred for his father who had killed his foster brother and taken his eye. Finnan had never met Ceallach's blood father, Ceirbeall, but looked forward to draining his blood on the field of battle. Maybe that was an honor best left for Ceallach, but it is a tall order for any man to kill his own father. Even if he did put a knife through your eye.

After a time, Finnan left Ceallach be and moved on, his thoughts were preoccupied also. Gormfhlaith had been left behind, as was to be expected, but Finnan had never spent more than a day or so away from her. He loved her, it was true, but that was of no importance to anyone, including him; he only thought about his duty to protect her.

And so they rolled on, each of them engrossed in their own thoughts. They made camp and dined together uneasily, and moved on again.

****

It was on the third night that Flaithbertach woke in the still dead of night and lay silent on the ground, listening through the darkness.

The long march had so far taken its toll on the soldiers and most were sleeping soundly.

The forest where they made camp was quiet. The train of men, wagons, and livestock had stopped haphazardly throughout and was scattered like the broken bones of a dead serpent.

They had been on the move for two days now and made slow progress through the thick ancient trunks of the old forest.

Flaithbertach turned onto his side and pushed himself up off the goatskin mat he had been sleeping on, his muscles sore from two days in the saddle and he had a late-night composing letters. He stood, letting his eyes adjust to the dim light of the tent, the fire was reduced to embers.

He felt the cold air on his face as he pulled back the flaps of the tent and made his way outside to relieve himself. A few soldiers wandered around but they took no notice of him.

He saw a Saxon slave girl sleeping outside his tent and knelt beside her to wake her gently. He beckoned her to follow.

The girl rose nervously, but without argument, and walked behind him toward the trees. He led her into the darkness of the forest, leaving the dimly lit camp behind them. He knew where they were going, he had been there before to pray and he was going to pray again tonight.

They walked for a few minutes in silence until they were well off the trail and out of earshot. Flaithbertach stopped before a great shadow and turned around to examine the girl. She let the garments fall about her legs and stood naked in front of him. She shivered from both the cold and fear, as Flaithbertach stared at her, his piercing, blue eyes bored into her very depths.

He took a step to the side as he slowly walked around her, she turned to match his gaze, unsure what was expected of her.

"Do you know what this place is?" Flaithbertach asked.

She recognized the Gaelic language, but did not understand his words and so made no answer.

"Not many people still worship the old Gods," he said, as he continued to circle her slowly, staring at her naked body. "They all follow the cross now. They follow monks like me. Men of the cloth." The last part, he spat out like a bad piece of meat. "Men of the cloth," he repeated. "The old Gods still have power, you know, you just have to know where to look."

He walked closer to her and stopped directly in front of her. He took her soft jaw in his strong right hand; he turned her head to one side. "Here," he said and gestured to the massive rocks either side of them. They were clearer now as their eyes adjusted to the darkness and some faint rays of moonlight broke through the clouds, highlighting the stones in a faint ghost-gray light.

"These stones have stood here for thousands of years, long before any Saxon, Viking, or Roman drew breath. Long before Jesus walked among men, these stones were placed here by my ancestors. They will stand here for thousands of years to come, long after you and I have turned to dust."

He was pleased with the one he had chosen and took a step back to gaze on her naked body again. He would have liked to take her and plant his seed inside her, but he was a disciplined man. He had chosen her for a reason. It was not a sacrifice if it was not something he wanted.

He stepped around her and planted his strong hands on her shoulders and pushed her forward from behind, under the great stone which straddled the two rocks supporting it from below.

This was a place of power, he knew, he could feel it as he started to recite the ancient incantation handed down through the druids of ancient by word of mouth from generation to generation.

He could feel the energy in the air as the hair on his arms stood. His Saxon companion felt it also, in arousal, she turned and pressed her body against his.

Flaithbertach's body responded, but his mind did not. He turned her again and ran his hands up along her body toward the top of her forehead, and held her head back with his left hand. With his right, he withdrew his sword, the darkness, he called it, as he continued his ancient Gaelic words.

She did not resist as she was under the influence of this place, its energy and his words hypnotized her as he drew the darkness to her throat. He pressed the point under the left edge of her jaw. The blade was sharp and did not need much pressure to open her soft skin. The blood sprayed for a brief moment, then reduced to a steady flow down her breasts and belly, onto the ancient stones below, as Flaithbertach drew across, opening her throat, and the girl gasped for air.

The old Gods would be pleased with his sacrifice and would surely help steer events in the direction he wished. He jerked her head back further to encourage the blood to flow, as the life faded from the body in his arms and into the stones around him.

Chapter Thirteen

Flan Sinna was up before dawn. His chambers were lit with candles as it was still two hours before sunrise. His breath fogged in the air as he walked naked, to the bronze pale of water, his bare feet cold on the flagstones. He upturned the pale over his head.

The water was freezing and instantly banished any grogginess from his mind. His thoughts, however, were troubled and the ever-present headaches were there, he had been dreaming just before he woke. Last night, he was addled by rumors of strife between Munster, ruled by his son-in-law Cormac, and Leinster. The kingdoms of Leinster were loyal to him, but loyalty was a fickle thing in this world.

The sky was cloudy on this cold September morning, he felt the need to get away for a while and clear his mind before putting the full weight of his thoughts to these rumors. He pulled on his woolen breeches and leather boots, and sat topless in the cold room, considering his day ahead. There was much to be done already. He did not have the patience for it today, patience was a thing of the past for him. He quickly stood and threw on his remaining clothes, pulling a heavy woolen cloak tight around him as he expected rain. It had rained every day for the last ten days. The thoughts of more rain upset him and he clenched his teeth as he set out.

The halls of his home were still basking in the silence of the morning, his were the only shadows moving about, flickering and dancing in the torchlight.

As he stepped outside, the first rays of sun were beginning to creep over the horizon, breaking through the clouds. He could hear a dog barking in the distance, the farmers would be starting to rise soon. He closed his eyes for moment, the headaches would get worse through the day. There was no sound, but the soft movement of the surrounding trees in the gentle breeze.

He walked around the back of the castle toward his kennels and stables, and nodded to the only soldier he passed. The yawning man, leaning against the stone walls quickly stiffened and stood up straight when he realized who it was walking toward him. The night watch would be turning in for breakfast soon, he thought he could get the faint smell of pork already. It was getting brighter and breakfast usually started at dawn for the night watch.

He thought about taking a morning ride, but he felt the need to stretch his legs instead, and pulled open the kennel doors. He stepped inside to be greeted by the sound of movement and yelping, as hounds jumped up on the sides of their wooden pen, eager to get out for the new day.

He took his favorite hound, Tintreach, and set out. The grounds were beginning to come to life as he stopped in the armory to pick up a hunting bow on the way to the gate, he did not want to lose out if he happened on a stag or a doe.

He had left his personal bow in his chambers. He didn't like using any weapon but his own, but he would not head back to the building, wasting time, and possibly bump into Padraig, his priest, who would be ranting on already about morning mass or MacGaman, his war chief, who always had a complaint or an issue to be addressed.

As he expected, the rain started as he and Tintreach wandered away from the castle walls, he had no destination in mind. It was light at first, but there was a damp smell in the air and dark clouds were closing in overhead, it was almost full daylight now and the birds started to sing.

Their walk took them on a cow trail through the fields, the animals were still grazing in the pastures and some of the farmers would be in the fields for milking about now. He would prefer to avoid them. It was still cold as the rain became heavier, turning to a steady hiss as they walked on together, Tintreach picked up scents here and there and dashed ahead, seemingly aimless, catching a scent and chasing some invisible creature, a badger, or rabbit, or fox, or God knows what.

They continued south, the sun, still low, tried in vain to break through the thick blanket of clouds to their left. His boots squelched in the trail below as it grew muddier with the rain which had been falling for an hour now.

He would soon need to turn back as there were peasants who wished to be seen regarding a land squabble which eventually led to a murder. He also wanted to get in sword practice and meet with his soldiers as he had a feeling trouble was brewing and would be at their gates before long. It was then, as if to reinforce his thoughts, that Tintreach started to bark at the sounds of a rider approaching. He knew that this would be nothing good.

****

Flan Sinna sat in silence over a breakfast of porridge and bread. He was a simple man and preferred the simple things in life.

"Ale," he said. "Bring me some ale." He knew the rider was not bringing good news. Riders never came with good news. "Who gave you this letter?" he asked the man. "Did you read it? The seal is broken."

"I did not read it, my Lord. The letter comes from the priest, Meonach," the messenger was nervous.

Flan took a spoon of porridge and looked up at the messenger again, "Who gave this to you?"

"Matudan. Cormac's War Chief."

Matudan. He remembered Matudan. "Why are you so nervous?" he roared at the messenger, who jumped. "What the hell are you so scared about? Get out," he shouted. "Get out."

The messenger stepped back, then hurried out.

Flan Sinna picked up the plate of porridge in front of him and flung it in the direction the man had gone, smearing white, gray porridge all over the stone wall in front of him.

The old priest who had married his daughter to Cormac. An ancient man who did not appear to have his wits about him, but who was a trusted advisor to the King of Munster.

What am I do with this? he thought, reading the contents. *I need council.* "Where is that God-forsaken ale?" he roared. "Send me the priest," he added. "I need advice."

He rose and walked to the window to look out at the cold summer's morning. *Why couldn't I just be left to walk and enjoy the sunshine,* he thought.

****

The priest arrived. "You sent for me, my King?" the young priest asked. His King stood, bent over a writing table, his shaggy red hair even more disheveled than usual. He turned suddenly, like a great bear about to pounce on a prey. "Read this," he demanded, and he threw the letter at the young priest.

The letter was written quickly but in a beautiful scrawl of Latin that came from an educated man. It was short and to the point. "My King," the priest read aloud, "Your daughter has been taken as a hostage by the monk, Flaithbertach. Your son-in-law will do little or nothing for her safe return until he has trodden his enemies in Leinster. I fear this will be too late for your daughter and my Queen. Ever faithful servant to the High King, Meonach, son of Duchais."

"You knew Meonach, priest," Flan declared. "Is it genuine? You knew Flaithbertach. Why would he do this?"

"My King," argued the priest, "I do not know. It is Meonach's seal, it must be the truth." And so after much debate, the high King of Ireland, Flan Sinna, gathered his men and his banner men and within a day, had eight-hundred strong, ready to march south to assist his son-in-law, if necessary, but more importantly, to free his daughter from the clutches of Flaithbertach.

****

The camp was a bustle of activity. Pigs squealed and hounds barked. The sun was up and soldiers were on the move, thousands of men traipsed here and there and trampled the dew-sodden ground to a muddy slick mess, horsemen mounted up and moved out, the animals whickered and snorted nervously, sensing the coming carnage, their breath fogged in the cool summer morning air.

There were men with their faces painted in various designs, blue and white and black. Some of these soldiers killed animals in the morning, chickens or sheep or goats as an offering. Pagan beliefs were still an influence in the Christian land. The blood of these animals was poured over their heads or spread across their faces.

Some men carried axes and some men carried short swords or maces, all men carried shields on their backs and spears by their side, their alternate weapon hung by their hip for close quarters. Only the chieftains and Kings wore any kind of heavy armor, the ordinary soldiers adorned in armor of black and brown leather, some wearing helmets which they had plundered in previous battles or traded with their meager savings.

Young boys, who were too young to fight, carried tall flags of all shapes and colors.

Within an hour, both sides faced each other across the battlefield. Cormac would speak with Ceirbeall first, riding out with Flaithbertach, Finnan, Torgny the Norseman, and Fogartach, King of Ciarraige, by his side. The small group of four riders stopped midway between the lines of troops; Flaithbertach holding a flag of truce, a cross on a white background, high for the enemy to see.

"They don't come, why don't they come?" Finnan asked.

"Wait," said Cormac, he sensed Finnan's eagerness to call out.

Flaithbertach waved the flag from side to side in the air and then planted it firmly in the ground below. They could see the faces of the men before them from this distance. Many of these men would die. Ceirbeall's army was outnumbered. The flags of the enemy flickered in the wind.

There was movement as some men rode forward, Cormac recognized the well-built figure of Ceirbeall, as he rode out on a great black horse, his son, Diarmuid, beside him, his ever-present spear in hand, as his cloak flapped in the wind behind him. Behind them were Ruarai Mac Ceirbeall, King of Osraigh, Cathal, King of Connaught, and Diarmuid's young son, Feidhlim, grandson to King Ceirbeall and nephew to Ceallach, a boy of just seventeen years.

The men met with silence between both armies. Thousands of men gathered, but a strange quietness held over them like a muffling blanket.

"You outnumber us," Ceirbeall started the conversation. "What are your terms?"

"We meet here as Kings," returned Cormac. "Yet, you show me little respect. My son is dead at your hands—"

"Foster son," interrupted Ceirbeall, "He was no blood to you. Retribution for the raids into my territory. You should be thankful you still have one foster son left alive."

"Ceallach, your own blood son you speak of?"

"He's no son of mine anymore," returned Ceirbeall, he sat tall on his black horse, his tattooed chest and arms displayed the ancient spiral designs of his forefathers. He stared at Cormac, through a face black with war paint, his hair was now shaved to the scalp, save for a short ponytail which he was letting grow down his back.

"We did not raid your territories," Cormac replied.

"Matters not at this stage, Cormac," Ceirbeall said. "We can make accusations and speak of this all night and day, it matters not. What matters is that we face each other across this field, ready to do great harm to each other." His horse shifted and he placed a large hand on her neck and rubbed her soothingly, "Now, I ask you again, what are your terms?"

After a moment's silence, Cormac raised a finger and said, "My son is dead, my other son, your own blood son." Diarmuid spat to one side at the mention of his blood brother's name. Cormac stared at him until the younger man dropped his gaze, "I want you, Ceirbeall. You will surrender to me and you will be hanged, and may God have mercy on your soul. Your young grandson, Feidhlim, son of Diarmuid here, will join me as my guest in Thomand, and your men will live. Diarmuid, Ruarai, and Cathal will swear fealty to me."

Diarmuid leaned over and spat again at this, Cathal also spat at the mention of his name. Cormac ignored them. "Your kingdom will be split in two," he continued, "divided between your son and a ruler of my choosing. These are the only terms I will accept. Take it or leave it. You die and your family, men, and kingdom live on, or you all die. Do what is right, Ceirbeall."

Ceirbeall and his men stared back in silence, Diarmuid gripped his spear tightly. "Who would you have rule my split kingdom?" Ceirbeall asked.

"Finnan will rule," replied Cormac.

Finnan turned and looked at Cormac. His face was calm, but his heart raced. He had been told nothing of this.

At that, Ceirbeall laughed out loud and urged his horse forward to get a better look at Finnan.

"This man? My heir, I greet you," he laughed again.

"A better chief than you," Cormac returned. "He will not murder or maim his children, I can guarantee you that."

Without another word, Ceirbeall turned and rode away, followed by his men.

"I think we have our answer," Flaithbertach said with a sigh. "He will never surrender and victory is not a sure thing for us, but we must fight. The raids will not stop. You have seen him, my King, it is the only way. Finnan, we disagree on most, but surely you must see that there is no talking to that man."

"There is no talking to him," Finnan said, as he turned his horse around. "On that we agree, Flaithbertach."

"We must fight," Fogartach put in. "Ceirbeall is a mad man. We outnumber them. We will win by the grace of God, there is no God in favor of a man who would maim his own son."

Flaithbertach lowered his head as he thought of the Lord, Jesus Christ, hanging from the cross, broken and dying at his father's bidding.

****

Gormfhlaith stood on the banks of the river as she looked across. It was morning and her bare feet were cold in the dewy ground. The mist was lifting like an army of angels soaring to the heavens.

As it cleared, a figure was unveiled on the other side of the river, still in shadow. "Gormfhlaith," it called in the familiar voice of her husband.

"Yes, my King, I am here," she said. She wanted to go to him.

"Gormfhlaith," he called again.

"I am here, my King. I will go to you," she said, and stepped closer to the river.

She could see him now. He stood on the far bank of the river, his hand was outstretched to her. She would go to him. His face was pained. He needed her.

"Farewell, my Queen," he said to her. "I must go now."

He turned slowly and began to walk away from the river, away from her. The birds were beginning to sing and the sun was starting to warm her face, as she walked through the damp grass, barefoot, toward the river. She stepped down the muddy bank toward the water, intending to wade across, she sensed it was shallow as she watched Cormac walk away, his back to her.

The water was not the icy cold water of the Munster rivers that should have greeted her, but warm. She looked down to see that it ran red and thick, as if she stood in a river of blood.

She tried to call to him, but her voice would not come to her. He stumbled as she watched him and fell to the ground out of sight.

"Cormac," she screamed. This time, she found her voice. It was dark as she sat alone in her quarters, still a few hours before sunrise. What did the dream mean? The river of blood. Her husband had called to her.

She rose and sat on the side of her bed, her bare feet touched the cold flagstones and it reminded her of the dewy grass by the stream and the contrast of the warm blood-filled river. She pulled her long hair back behind her neck and tied it, then rested her elbows on her knees and laid her eye sockets on her warm open palms.

"My Queen," a voice called from outside the room. "My Queen, I heard you scream. May I come in?"

"Yes, Niamh," she replied to her servant. "And light my room. What has you up at this hour?"

The young woman entered and set a candle down on the wooden table beside her bed, and handed Gormfhlaith a goatskin fleece to pull around her. There was a chill in the air and the animal hair felt good on her skin. Niamh then busied herself with the rest of the candles in the room and set to work, getting the fire going as she spoke.

"There was a messenger in the night, my Queen. Carrying a letter bearing the seal of Flaithbertach, son of Inmainén."

"A message from Flaithbertach?" the Queen repeated. The dream which woke her was receding to broken fragments in the back of her mind now, but it still bothered her. *Cormac,* she thought. "What has happened," she whispered to herself.

"My Queen?" questioned Niamh.

"Why did you not wake me, Niamh? Where is the message?"

Gormfhlaith stood and downed a pitcher of water which had been on her table. "Prepare my clothes and bring me the message. Never mind the fire. It can wait. And bring me something to eat," she said.

She was worried and irritable, and had a bad feeling about this message. Dark tidings from the dark monk. Flaithbertach was not in her good graces. She had been against marching on Leinster, but Flaithbertach had insisted. The King obviously valued his council over hers. And now, here was a message from Flaithbertach in the dead of night. It could not be good news.

And her dream, what had it meant? She could not remember now. Cormac. She had been trying to get to him.

As she waited for Niamh to bring her clothes, she placed her chair on the middle of the bearskin mat in the center of her room and dropped to her knees to place her elbows on the chair. She faced the wooden cross that hung on the wall and joined her hands to pray.

An hour later, the sun began to rise, the first cracks of sunlight made their way through the candlelit halls of Thomand. Gormfhlaith was seated in her seat of office, her husband's empty seat beside her.

She held the rolled paper in her hand and studied the wax seal, as she contemplated what was written inside. Strict orders to the messenger from Flaithbertach, that it be delivered to the Queen and opened by her and her only. The messenger, a Munsterman whom she did not know, stood before her, as did Muirichain, the head of her personal guard while Finnan was away. She wished Finnan was here.

She broke the seal and unrolled the parchment to reveal the monk's handwriting.

"My Queen," began the letter. "I write to you with haste and urgency that you may heed this letter and come without delay to your King's aid."

Cormac needs me, she thought, the remnants of a forgotten dream from that morning crept back.

She continued to read, "It is with great difficulty that I implore you to come, for I do not wish to put you in harm's way, and I fear I will anger my King by my actions. He would not have you near the danger of the battleground."

She gripped the parchment tighter as she read, "His mind is elsewhere. His mood is bothered. He is not himself. I fear for his judgment and the decisions he will make without strength by his side. I can only steer him so much. I beg you to take your guards and ride with all haste with my messenger, to make camp with us, and stand by your husband's side."

The bottom of the parchment was signed off, "Your faithful servant, Flaithbertach."

****

The forest was black, save for the flickering torches and the fires of the makeshift camp. Five horses and five riders, one of them, a Queen. Gormfhlaith traveled with little extravagance. Speed was of the essence. She rode her horse, like a common soldier, no carriage, and she sat among her guards at the campfire.

She had wanted to travel throughout the night, but her guards insisted that this was impossible and would result in the injury of one or more of the horses slowing them down further. It was not worth the ground they could gain.

She sat by the fire, the light reflected softly on her face as she warmed herself and ate a piece of chicken with some onions put together by Muirichain. He was as handy a cook as he was a soldier. A somber man of about forty years, he had insisted that it was madness riding out to the countryside where cattle raids were rampant. Norsemen could come out of anywhere and worse, the destination of intent was a battleground where the decimation of the kingdom she represented was entirely possible.

"Why must you leave, my Queen?" Muirichain had asked. "What could be so urgent and what difference will you make? Finnan was clear. I am to protect you. How can I protect you out here? How can I protect you in a battleground? Have you ever even—"

She slapped her hand on the table where she had sat after reading the letter from Flaithbertach, "You can't take care of me? Well, then what use are you to me? I will be leaving in the morning, whether you are with me or not, Muirichain."

They argued for an hour or more. The dour soldier pleaded with her. He threatened to lock her up, he threatened to inform the King, threats which she laughed at.

"You'll lock me up? You personally will lock me up? Then the men behind you will simply unlock it because I am their Queen. Your Queen, Muirichain. And yes, feel free to tell Cormac. You'll be there right next to me. So, either I will leave in the morning without you, or I will leave under your protection, but one way or the other, I will be leaving at sunrise."

Muirichain sighed and agreed. He picked three of his best men from what was left to guard the town from any possible attack, and the small group departed at sunrise at the insistence of the stubborn Queen.

"What do you expect to gain, my Queen?" Muirichain asked, as they sat by the fire. Two men stood guard, the other, a one-armed man named Murchu, who still managed to ride a horse, had fallen asleep by the fire.

"God help us, I can't wait to have Finnan back. The man doesn't speak, you know. He refuses to speak. The silence used to madden me, but you know what? I'd take it over your incessant questions any day."

"My Queen—"

"BAH!" she shouted, and spat in the fire, sleeping rough with these men was changing her into one of them, she thought. "Would you question your King? Would you even open your mouth to him without permission?"

"I would not. But I'm the chief here when the whole Godforsaken army of Munster has left us."

"Godforsaken," she said. "I hope not."

"Anyway, they're gone and when they're gone, I'm your right-hand man and I owe it to you and to my King, and to Finnan."

"To Finnan?" she asked, her face reddened.

"Yes – to everybody," he said. "I owe it to everybody to keep you safe and to point out when you're doing something stupid, irresponsible, stubborn—"

"I see, I see, you have made your point, you are free to speak and express your opinion and it is valued," she said, and threw the bones of chicken into the fire and watched them crackle. She then watched Muirichain as he cracked open his own chicken bones and sucked the marrow out of them.

"Yes, valued, but not heeded. Pointless!" he said, and threw the remainder of his bones in the fire. "Pointless," he said again, as he stared at her.

"It's not going to change. Not now," she said.

"Anyway, my Queen," he said with more respect, he had forgotten in the last two days, he was dealing with his Queen, as her stubbornness made her seem a child to him. "What do you expect to gain?"

"Flaithbertach says he needs me. He pleaded with me to come. I showed you the letter."

"And I told you what I thought of it," Muirichain said, he rose and stretched. "You go because the black monk sends for you?"

"He did not send for me. He asked for me. He asked my assistance."

"And when have the two of you ever seen eye to eye? When have you ever trusted him?"

"Never," she replied. "I do not like the man."

"Then—"

"We've been through it," she cut him off. "Over and over and over. This is the end of it, Muirichain. We are done," she was shouting now, the one-armed man woke and sat up. He said nothing, but got up and walked to the bushes, and they heard the hiss of urine on the undergrowth.

"As you wish, my Queen. I am sorry. Finnan does not trust him so therefore, I do not trust him. You will have my sword at your side at all times, my lady. You should get some sleep."

If there was anyone out there, the small group would have made themselves known, the sounds of their argument probably traveled for miles through the forest, but nothing stirred apart from the animals of the night.

Gormfhlaith woke before dawn to the sound of wood splintering, as one of the men laid into some logs with an axe. "My lady, I did not mean to wake you. It is still early. You can sleep some more."

"No matter, Muirichain," she got up and drank down some water. It was her habit in the morning. Sometimes, it was ale or wine if her husband had some in the chamber, but it was usually water. "I need to do some woman business," she told them. "Keep your distance."

She squatted in the trees and listened to the birds twittering in the dappled light under the canopy, as the first rays of sunlight broke their way through the branches. A mouse scuttled past under foot. "No worries, little mouse," she said. Oh, to be a mouse and leave the politics of being a Queen far behind. She had wished so many times that she was not a Queen and that she was free to work as she wished. She would work the land maybe. Or fish. That would be nice too. To sit by a cow and milk her in the morning, in her own little farm, and then go and have breakfast in her little house on a dirt floor, with a husband of her choosing, one who could give her children. She sighed and rose. She loved Cormac, but she had no freedom and no future. Her bloodline was finished.

"My Queen," called a voice from the camp.

"I'm coming," she said, and made her way back.

"My Queen," he said again.

The old fool was going deaf, she thought, and shouted this time, "I'm coming!!" She instantly regretted her demeanor. Muirichain was a loyal soldier and restless in making sure all was in order. Nothing slipped past him. She could see why he was left in charge, in Finnan's absence.

"I'm sorry. I'm worried," she said.

"Nothing to be sorry for." Everything was ready to go. After a quick breakfast of apples and some bread, they mounted their horses and headed out, and broke free from the oppressive, dark canopy of the forest around noon.

They rode throughout the day and caught their first glimpse of the camp fires shortly after dawn the next day. It was mostly non-fighting folk they came into contact with first on the outskirts of the canvas city. They did not recognize her in the dark, she was just another rider with some soldiers. It was not until they were further toward the center of the camp that they were questioned in the golden light of the dawn. She pulled back her hood to let the man see who it was. The cold breeze ruffled her hair

"The Queen has arrived," the man called. "My lady," he greeted her and took the reins of her horse and led them into the camp.

"What news?" Muirichain asked.

"No point in asking me. Terms were given, but I know of no response. We meet again today."

"I will see the King now," Gormfhlaith said.

"The King is sleeping, my lady. Maybe some breakfast first?"

"We've eaten," she said. "I will see the King now, sleeping or not."

The man led them into the camp, past a group of merchants unloading their wares, sacks of grain, and bags of vegetables from a rickety wooden cart which looked like it had barely made the journey. They carried on further, past tents erected here and there. Soldiers, likely scouts, were returning, tired and irritable and ready for sleep, wandered past them, a priest prayed on his knees, a young man, maybe one of Meonach's group. They rode on and dismounted by a canvas tent, with stacks of hay lined up outside.

Their horses were taken inside, fed, and cleaned. The soldiers found some hot water where they could bathe and Muirichain and Gormfhlaith accompanied the man who had greeted them to the King's tent.

"I leave you here, my lady."

"What is this?" a voice came from behind them. Finnan marched forward, wearing his wool undergarments, his hair was wet and a sword hung by his side. "My lady, what are you doing here? Why have you come?"

She sighed and rolled her eyes. She had hoped to avoid him for as much of her stay as possible. Wishful thinking.

"Muirichain, you will explain this to me in private. What is wrong with you?" Finnan demanded. "You have brought your Queen to the battlefield?"

"Don't blame him," Gormfhlaith said. "I gave him no choice. I would have come regardless."

"Why come here? Why?" he stood close to her and in a low voice, said, "Do you realize where you are, Gormfhlaith? Do you realize the danger you are in here? What prompted this madness?"

"I gave you no leave to address me in the familiar," she said in Latin. "He needs me."

"He needs you. How do you know?" Finnan ground his teeth hard enough to wear them down, but spoke quietly.

"I dreamed of it," she said, switching back to Gaelic for the sake of Muirichain. She looked him straight in the eye and gave a slight shake of her head. Finnan could not know of Flaithbertach's involvement.

Finnan held his cool. "Everybody back to work," he said. "Muirichain, I will come and find you." The soldiers dispersed. "You too," he said to the two men standing outside Cormac's tent. "Get away," he waved his hand in the air to dismiss them. "Go talk to him then," he told her. She looked at him, sadness in her eyes. She wanted to tell him, but couldn't. It would not help matters. "Go," he said again.

Finnan walked her to the tent and pulled the flap back for her to enter, then moved to a respectful distance. The King would send for him if it was required.

He sat on the ground and took his sword in his lap and began to sharpen the blade, running the stone along its edge over and over.

"Something vexes you?" a voice came from behind him.

He turned and saw Flaithbertach.

"I'm in no mood for you, priest," Finnan said.

"I'm not a priest," the monk replied. "Who is with the King?" he asked.

"Not your concern," Finnan replied, he did not look at the monk. Flaithbertach stood next to Finnan and smiled, with his hand over his eyes, shielding his gaze from the morning sun.

"As you wish, Finnan. I ask only out of concern." He turned to leave, and paused before turning back to Finnan, "We do not need to argue all of the time, Finnan. We are on the same side here." There was only one person who could get him that worked up, Flaithbertach thought, the Queen had arrived. The chess piece was in place. There was one final item Flaithbertach would need to attend to.

****

Diarmuid rose at dawn. Yesterday, his father had laughed Cormac Mac Cuileneann and his terms of surrender off the field which divided the two armies. Their terms were acceptable to Diarmuid, offering to make him a chieftain which was more than he was now, but his loyalty to his father was strong. Loyalty coupled with a healthy fear of retribution.

He buried his head in the same drinking trough his horse was guzzling from, and threw on a saddle. He jumped on, his head still wet. The summer morning air was still cold as he secured his spear by his back and turned to ride out, he left the camp to ride northeast.

"Less than a day's ride," he had been assured by the mad monk. The High King of Ireland would be coming for them. He had no idea how Flaithbertach had convinced Flan Sinna to ride south, but this is what he was led to believe, and this is what his father believed.

"Why will he side with us against his son-in-law?" Ceirbeall had asked the mad monk.

"Do you play chess, Ceirbeall?" the mad monk had asked.

"Chess?" Ceirbeall was more of a warrior than a game's man. "I do not play games, priest. What of it?" he demanded.

"A shame," Flaithbertach replied. "To exercise the mind is just as important as the body, maybe that is why you need my help to defeat Cormac." Flaithbertach smiled, that black smile of his. He smiled and sipped at his wine in the halls of Leinster all those months ago, his finger still pumping blood where he had torn it off in an effort to convince Ceallach's brother that Flaithbertach was one of them.

"Priest, explain yourself quickly before I have more than your finger removed," Ceirbeall had responded in irritation.

"The Queen," Flaithbertach had said, "is the most powerful piece on the chessboard. That is how we make Flan Sinna fight for us. We move out our Queen from the back ranks."

"Priest, you speak in riddles, but if you can make Flan Sinna join us, then I'll be impressed."

"He will come," Flaithbertach said. "I can make it happen."

Diarmuid rode on, his hair was drying in the morning sun, he looked back to view the two camps, the future battleground spread wide between them, morning campfires burned, the smell of meat rose from cook stations scattered throughout. Livestock were grazing, sheep, cattle, goats, chickens here and there. He could hear a cock crowing and a dog barking.

The sun snuck out from behind the clouds for a moment, forcing him to raise his arm to shield his eyes, as he looked over the camps below.

He turned his horse and rode on, along a trampled cow trail. He sped through the heather at a gallop and only slowed when the trees became thicker. He entered an evergreen forest and came to a trot, ducking low to avoid branches here and there.

He rode for the best part of the morning, his plan was to ride until sundown and wait a day if necessary. If the two armies were to meet now, both sides would be decimated. There could be no winners, but his father would not back down, and in truth, neither would he if it were his decision.

Diarmuid dismounted at a shallow river to let his horse drink. He stripped to the waist, waded in shin deep, and dropped to his hunkers to throw water over his head.

As the cool water dripped down his neck and back, he felt someone's eyes bore into him from behind. His spear was with his horse five paces away, but no matter, if these weren't the people he was looking for, then they were no threat to him. He turned and searched through the thick covering of trees on the river bank, but saw nothing. He knew somebody was there, the birds had fallen silent, and there was not a sound. It was too quiet.

"Come on, step out," he called. "I'm alone, my weapons are with my horse. I can't hurt you," the silence continued.

He turned to walk to his horse.

"Easy," a voice called. "That's right. You can't hurt us. We have an arrow on you, we'll lose if you don't stop. That's it, nice and slow now." The voice continued, "What brings you out here?"

"You," Diarmuid answered, not turning, extending his arms slowly.

"Me?" he could hear the smile in the voice. "How in the hell would you have business with me? I'm just a voice in the trees."

Diarmuid had to smile in turn, "Yes, not you personally. Your King. You're one of Flan's men."

"How would you know that now?" the voice materialized from the other side of the stream, a grizzled old warrior, stocky, with a short sword on one hip and an axe on the other, he carried a wooden staff in his two hands, taller than himself. He landed with a splash as he jumped from the small bank a short distance from Diarmuid. He was accompanied by a hooded bowman who held a bow and arrow in place, aimed at Diarmuid, ready to lose.

Two other men accompanied them, their gazes fixed waiting for Diarmuid to make the wrong move. "Speak or my Norse friend here will put an arrow through your face."

"I'm not a Norseman," the skinny man with the bow replied in a strange accent, Diarmuid noticed the array of religious paraphernalia hanging from his neck. A cross, a Nordic hammer, and other artifacts he did not recognize.

"I know why you ride south with an army," Diarmuid said. "And I'm here to help."

"Help how? Speak quickly, my friend here, his arm tires."

"It does," the bowman agreed.

"The Queen, Gormfhlaith. She has been taken. I'm here to guarantee her return."

"Well then," said the lead man leaning on his staff in the water, "you better be coming with us to see the King."

The man's name, Diarmuid learned, was MacGaman, he was scouting the woods when they came across Diarmuid. They were camped a half a day's ride away and the King had, as Flaithbertach promised he would, ridden with an army that would turn the tide in the coming battle in the favor of whoever they could be convinced to join.

"So you're Diarmuid, son of Ceirbeall?" MacGaman asked. "Son of the King of Leinster?"

"I am," Diarmuid replied.

"Best spearman in all the south?"

"Maybe. Do you want to test me?"

"Aye, I do," replied MacGaman, "but not before you've spoken to him." They rode on in silence for a long time before arriving at the outskirts of the camp beside a river of clean-running water. A crowd was gathered as they rode in, watching a contest of some sort, cheering, and shouting.

Flags of green and red surrounded the camp and rippled in the gentle breeze, smoke rose lazily from the campfires scattered throughout.

Diarmuid could hear the soft thud of bodies falling in the damp muddy ground and the crowd spread at the arrival of the horsemen to reveal a stout, sturdy looking man of middle age, with wild red hair, and a huge beard caked from head to toe in muck, as he pounded the face of another man with his closed fist. It was hard to tell the difference between blood and mud as the man raised his fist and brought it down with such force that the victim must surely be dead, for his face was a soft, slick mess.

The bearded man let the soon-to-be corpse drop from his arms, like a bag of wet meat and turned to face the newcomers, his eyes were ablaze with a fire that would put fear in the hardiest of Norsemen.

"My King," MacGaman greeted the fighter, "you will want to speak to this man. He brings news of your daughter."

"In my tent," roared the King. "And who is he that you trust so much that he's not in chains?"

No explanation was offered for the spectacle Diarmuid had witnessed, and without a word or argument, he was placed in chains and led to the King's tent, while Flan Sinna walked to the river to wash the mud and blood from his body.

He arrived to his tent naked and stood before the kneeling Diarmuid, drying his red mane, "My daughter has been taken. By a mad monk from what I hear. Flaithbertach. I have met the man before. I'm told my son-in-law does little or nothing to help us?" He threw the towel on the ground and a slave girl removed it. "Who are you?" Flan Sinna asked, staring at Diarmuid.

"I am Diarmuid, son of Ceirbeall."

"You saw what I did to that man outside?"

"I did," replied Diarmuid.

"And yet you, the enemy of my son-in-law and daughter, rode directly to find me? Are we not at odds with each other, Diarmuid?" the red-haired King asked, as he sat before the burning fire and wrapped a blanket around himself.

"We are not. I can guarantee your daughter's safety. Flaithbertach will release her."

"For you? For his enemy? You better start making sense soon, man, or I swear to you this will not work out so good for you," he said, as he rubbed his bruised knuckles.

"Perhaps you can remove the chains first so we can have a proper discussion?" Diarmuid asked, holding his hands out before him.

"I could, but I won't," he pointed to a candle with a bruised and bloodied forefinger. It was burning low in the corner. "We have conversed long enough, my friend. You will now speak and convince me, and if you don't have me convinced by the time that candle has burned out, you will float down the river in pieces. Understand?"

Flan Sinna sat back, his naked form displayed under the towel was enough to make any man uneasy.

"Yes," said Diarmuid. "I am to believe your daughter rode to her husband, to convince him of the foolishness of his battle against us. The wasted life."

"Cormac is a man of peace," Flan replied. "The candle is burning."

"He is that, but he seeks peace with the Norsemen in the east."

Flan rose an eyebrow.

"Proof," he said.

"We have the proof. We have a letter, bearing Cormac's seal. We cannot have friends of the Norsemen at our borders. I do not know what he is thinking, but we cannot have this. Surely you must see that?"

Flan did not respond, but arched back to glance over his shoulder at the burning candle.

"Flaithbertach hates the Vikings and in his haste to change Cormac's mind, he took your daughter and threatened her life. He would kill her if a treaty with the Norsemen was written. Cormac will not back down," Diarmuid continued. "His treaty with the Norsemen is more important than his wife. Help us to help you. Flaithbertach will treat with my father. He will speak with him."

"Indeed," said Flan, and the candle burned out. He stood in the gloom, then carried a flame from the fire to light the torches about the tent. He looked like a crazed monk as he wandered about, with his red hair and beard protruding from all angles.

"What are your terms?"

"Fight with us. Stop Cormac. Let us rule Thomand in his stead."

"MacGaman, get rid of the chains and have him cleaned and fed. He will ride with us. We break camp now."

"Cormac is to live," Flan said, as Diarmuid was helped to his feet.

"My father will agree if you leave the punishment of Flaithbertach to us."

"You expect me to let the man who took my daughter get away with it?"

"No, I don't, I simply ask that you let us decide what a fitting punishment is for him. Flaithbertach has a reputation of insanity and harshness, but he acted in good faith for the Gaelic of this land. He did this to avoid giving strength to the Norsemen."

Flan handed Diarmuid a cup of wine as the voices outside told of the preparations for the army to get moving, "We will see."

****

115

Gormfhlaith had found Cormac in a sound sleep, his breath was deep and even, his complexion was healthy. He looked good and she was surprised.

She had sat with him in silence for a while. He was tired. She could tell from the depth of his breathing, but slept soundly and his mind was at ease.

She poured herself a glass of ale and crossed the tent to his writing table. His thoughts were recorded here and as she read, she saw only signs of confidence. If Flan Sinna, her father, could be convinced to join them, they could leave this field with no bloodshed. Why then had the monk sent for her?

He woke an hour after dawn. "Gormfhlaith, why are you here?" his voice was urgent, his eyes bright. He sat up on his bed and rubbed his eyes hard, wondering if he were dreaming.

"I was worried," she replied in Latin. "I dreamed you would not return."

I may not, he thought to himself. "Gormfhlaith, this is a dangerous place you have come to." He stood and walked to her, with his arms wide to embrace her, "Dreams, Gormfhlaith, why would you come based on a dream?"

"You have based this whole war on a dream," she shouted. "What are you talking about? I thought you were unwell. I thought your mind was addled, that you weren't yourself."

He shushed her and rocked her gently in his arms. "Is that what you dreamed?" he asked her. She did not answer. Why had the black monk sent for her? "We need to get you home in the morning," he spoke softly. "Come, sit with me." She cried. She was afraid to mention the letter. They sat together as she cried.

The day passed and the sun came out and she slept for some of it. The King was busy, making plans, meeting with his chiefs, inspecting soldiers, seeing to preparations for a battle which he hoped would not take place.

A few hours before dawn the next morning, the camp was chaos, as men went here and there to prepare weapons and armor, stable boys readied horses, hurried breakfasts were eaten, and mass was given. The camp emptied, save for a few soldiers, tradesmen, and prostitutes.

Cormac and his army rode out once more to offer renewed terms to the King of Leinster. Gormfhlaith had been left in the company of Muirichain and two other guards in Finnan's absence, she dined on beef stew in Cormac's tent, while her guards waited outside. The stew did not sit well, her stomach was unsettled. She paced back and forth.

"My Queen," a voice came from outside. "It is Flaithbertach. Will you see him?"

"I will," she said. Why was he not with the King?

The monk entered, "May I sit?"

His eyes, darker than usual, she thought, were fixed on her.

He was a different man from the brown-robed monk who walked quietly around the halls of Thomand. Over his brown undergarments, he wore a leather armored vest and a black wool cloak over this. A wooden shield with a white bird on a dark background adorned his back and by his side hung a short sword and an axe.

"Why did you send for me, Flaithbertach? It seems I have made things worse for my King. Why have you sent for me?"

He sat beside her as she lay on the bed, eying her through his black eyes and great black beard. He remained silent. *His eyes are so dark*, she thought. *Didn't he always have blue eyes?* Her anger pushed aside the irrelevant thought. "I did not give you leave to sit, did I?" she asked, raising her voice.

"My Queen," he said. "Gormfhlaith. My Queen."

This isn't right. "Muirichain," she called.

Muirichain entered, his brow was wrinkled in concern. "Show him out. He is no longer welcome."

"My Queen," Muirichain said in agreement. "Flaithbertach, please."

Flaithbertach rose and stepped outside with Muirichain. "What did you say to her?" Muirichain's voice was rough, "How did you offend her?"

"I did not say anything," Flaithbertach answered, as he loosened his axe from his side. He raised it quickly and caught Muirichain hard under the chin with the back of the axe, splitting the man's lower jaw in two before he even realized what was happening. Blood gushed to the ground, it blended with the dirt in the gloom of the dawn.

The other two soldiers guarding the tent heard the commotion, one of them drew his sword and ran to Flaithbertach, and the other ran to the Queen, shouting in panic.

Flaithbertach looked up at the approaching soldier, he was a young man, his face was anxious. Flaithbertach took stock and threw the axe. It caught him in the side of the head, crunching through his skull.

He knelt over Muirichain. "A new era is dawning, my friend," Flaithbertach said, as he held his sword to his chest, before driving the blade through his ribcage and into his heart. Blood bubbled out of the old warrior's mouth and his eyes glazed over as he died. Flaithbertach rose and entered the Queen's tent to take care of the second soldier.

****

Cormac sat atop his white horse behind lines of Gaelic warriors, carrying axes and swords to fight for him, as Flaithbertach rode thunderously up and down the front ranks in a battle frenzy as he rallied the troops. The men roared and beat their shields, they swore oaths of death and destruction on the enemy and screamed in rage.

Around three-thousand men had marched with him from Munster and another thousand had come to join him from other parts. He counted the banners before him, dotted throughout the men, and noted each family and group. Some, he was surprised, had showed to fight for him – Flaithbertach had recruited many and convinced them to join his cause, his Norse mercenaries included.

The soldiers were on foot, armed with axes and swords and spears, protected by their wooden shields. Some carried a spare shield across their backs.

Only the Kings and war chiefs sat on horses. Many would dismount to fight. Some had brought war chariots with them. There were forty-eight in total.

It was a cold morning for the summer, Cormac could see the fog from his horse's breath forming in the air before him as he shivered, thinking about what was before him. Four thousand men against the three and a half thousand Ceirbeall had in front of him.

He watched as Flaithbertach rode past the front ranks, screaming words of encouragement, as the soldiers responded with screams and shouts of their own. He was riding his black stallion hard up and down in such a frenzy that his horse stopped and bucked, throwing the monk to the ground. The horse raised its front hoof gingerly then lowered to its front knees.

Cormac winced when he heard the jeers from the opposing side. Flaithbertach got back up, but there was an unnerving silence from his men. A movement to his right caught Cormac's eye and he saw one of the banners shift. A few men emerged from the battle group and left the field.

"Where are you going?" screamed Flaithbertach. "Where are you going?" he screamed again. He marched up and down in disarray, his face and beard were splattered with mud where he had fallen, and his nose was bloodied.

"You are deserting your King," he shouted.

More men filed away from either side of Cormac.

"Stop," shouted Flaithbertach. "Stop. Cowards. Where are you going? Do not desert your King!"

Cormac could see this was no use. It was surely a bad omen for a holy man to fall from his horse just before the battle. A stream of men filed from the army, like blood streaming from a wounded beast, as Flaithbertach screamed at them like a madman.

"Filthy cowards," Flaithbertach shouted, as he marched back toward the stricken horse.

He took out the darkness, sharpened for battle, as the animal whickered and struggled to get up.

Cormac was transfixed by what he was seeing. Streams of men were still turning and walking away. Hundreds had turned, maybe even a thousand. Mostly men Flaithbertach had recruited, judging from the banners he had seen. Most of Cormac's loyal men remained, but this display of madness from Flaithbertach was not helping matters.

"We need to get him out of there," Finnan said, and spurred his horse forward. Flaithbertach screamed at the horse and raised his sword to bring it down on the animal's neck, cutting it wide open. The animal bucked and spasmed, blood spurted from the gaping hole. Before Finnan could get to him, Flaithbertach raised his sword again and hacked the stallion's head clean off. The headless body spasmed and kicked as Finnan reached Flaithbertach.

More and more men streamed away, shaking their heads, their spears were held low. *Who would want to fight for a madman,* Cormac thought, as he saw some of the men loyal to him join the deserters. He spurred his horse on and galloped back and forth. "Do not flee," he implored them, but he saw the downcast eyes of those who broke rank. The damage was done. He could not appear weak now by begging. He must not. He must appear strong even if his right hand was in disarray.

Flaithbertach stood above the butchered animal with his sword held low in a shaking hand, blood stained his pale, sweating face and cloak.

"Flaithbertach," called Finnan. "What have you done?"

He jumped from his horse and grabbed the abbot tightly by the arm.

"What is wrong with you?" demanded Finnan. "Have you lost your mind? Look what you have done. Come, we need to go."

"Cowards," said Flaithbertach. He spat as he shook off Finnan's grip and marched toward the soldiers, the men parted like the Red Sea for Moses, as he made for the camp.

Cormac watched Flaithbertach leave, as he guided his horse toward Finnan.

"What was that?" asked the younger man. "He has lost his mind – and a third of our army. That is on him, Cormac."

"He fell, Finnan. There is nothing to be done for it now," replied Cormac, but he knew his friend's actions had severely damaged their cause. "I must address the men," Cormac said, and turned. What could he say to put the fighting heart back into these soldiers after what they had just seen?

"I am Cormac Mac Cuileneann, Bishop and King of Munster," he shouted. "I am a holy and just man, and I am your King," he continued. His face was red from the force of his voice and his throat already raw. "You watched those men leave the field of battle. Why do we need men like that?" he shouted, as he drew his sword. His old voice was hoarse but it could not fail him now, "Is it not better that we see them leave now and not on the field of battle when we are fighting for our lives?" At this, some of the men cheered.

"Is it not better that you know that the man standing next to you right here, right now, will not desert you?" He raised his sword in the air, "Look at him now. He will not leave you. That man will stand beside you, spear in hand, and protect you like a brother, as you protect him."

Men shouted in answer to his words, their jaws set. Some banged their spears and swords against their shields and others raised their fists to the air and screamed with bloodlust. He brought his horse to a halt and dismounted, handing the reins to Finnan, "I am Cormac Mac Cuileneann, your King, and as you have stood with me, I will kneel for you." He dropped to one knee and raised his sword in homage to the men before him.

This was met with a rapturous cheer from the men of Munster in front of him and a thunderous sound as they beat their shields with spear, sword, and axe, and chanted the name of their King. Their shouts continued as Cormac remounted, only to be drowned out by the sound of a horn across the way.

He turned to look west across what would potentially be the bloody battlefield, to see more warriors spilling down the hills, joining the ranks of his enemy. Hundreds of men, horses, and chariots spilled over the hill to the booming, monotonous tone of war horns. The enemy force swelled in number, as Cormac saw the black cross of Flan Sinna, the High King of Ireland, as it was carried down the field of battle to face him. His father-in-law had arrived and stood with his enemy.

****

Darkness was falling as Cormac returned to the encampment, torches flickering through the gathering dusk as he found his way to his tent. They could not fight and hope to win, he thought. They were heavily outnumbered.

Why is Flan Sinna here? he thought, as he dismounted and handed his reigns to Alfred. He had hoped to seek Flans' help but here he was joined with Ceribeall's Army.

His feet squelched through the mucky ground as he walked past the scattered campfires.

He could see a soft glow from the entrance of his tent as he approached and welcomed the thoughts of warming his old body in silent meditation on the decisions he would be making tomorrow.

"My wife must not know of her father's arrival" he said to Finnan. "Get her ready. See that she leaves before sunrise. Take twenty of your best men and escort her back to Thomand."

"My King, travel by night is dangerous – can we spare the men?"

"To hell with the men, Finnan," Cormac shouted, he buried his face in his hands and rubbed his eyes. "If we fight tomorrow, we will be defeated. Twenty men will make no difference. Keep her safe. She is in a den of snakes here and must not stay. She must not," he hissed. "Attend to it now. We will negotiate in the morning and come what may, but she will be safe."

Cormac pulled Finnan toward him and held him tight for an instant.

"Get her to safety," Cormac whispered, with a squeeze of Finnan's shoulder. "Get her away from here," he said, as he stepped under the flap of his tent.

It took a moment for his eyes to adjust to the gloom. As they did, he noticed a figure crouched, like a dark statue in the corner, staring at the ground.

"Flaithbertach. Not now, Flaithbertach. I need to be alone. Not now."

"Now," came the whispered answer. "Now. You owe me that much, Cormac," he said.

Cormac sighed, but did not have the energy to reproach him for addressing him in the familiar.

"You owe me. You said we would fight. You said we would take these lands. You said we would spread the word of God."

Silence followed as Cormac sat, the firelight dancing off their faces. Flaithbertach would not meet his gaze, but stared into the flames.

"What was that out there? What happened to you? You appeared as a madman."

"What was that?!" shouted Flaithbertach, jumping to his feet, spit dribbled down his beard as he faced Cormac, the flames reflecting in his intense, black eyes. "What was that? That was a man ready to fight and die for his King. I will follow you to the ends of the earth, Cormac. I will follow you into battle tomorrow. We do not need the cowards who fled, we do not need them."

The cowards that fled because of your questionable actions, Cormac thought grimly. He sat. "I cannot do this now, Flaithbertach," he said, as he buried his face in the warmth of the palms of his hands, seeking darkness and solitude. "It is a fight we cannot win. Flan Sinna has come from the north. He has joined Ceirbeall's army. We are outnumbered at least two to one."

"Flan will not fight his son-in-law," Flaithbertach said. "Attack at first light and we have the advantage on them. Form up at dawn and cut them open as they ready themselves. Do this for me, Cormac. You owe me this battle," he roared, not caring who heard them argue. He paced up and down, kicking the dusty ground as he marched, his eyes ablaze, flickering in the firelight with madness.

"You forget yourself, Flaithbertach," Cormac said coldly. "I am your King, and you will address me accordingly. I owe you nothing. I will help you where I can, but I will not march our army to their death."

With that, Flaithbertach stopped and turned, walking back toward the brazier. He trembled as he faced Cormac. "Then, my King" he said, nose to nose with Cormac, the smell of wine from his breath reaching Cormac, "you are as big a coward as those who fled." He turned and left.

****

Ceallach was dead. Every man was dead before a battle, as they stood with sword and shield in hand, staring at their foe across the field. The battle gave them life again as they spilled blood to quench the thirst of the ground below. This gave men life. There was nowhere more alive than the battlefield.

Ceallach was dead, but as soon as he charged, sword and shield in hand, he would live again, until he was cut down or until he found his father and took his head from his shoulders, after he tore his eyes from their sockets with his bare hands.

His torn eye pained him and his head ached horribly since he had woken on a bed in Thomand a month before. He had succumbed to bouts of shaking twice since then and blacked out only to wake sometime after, weak and addled. This remained his secret.

He was glad to be at the front lines, to be present for the maddening clash of bone and steel as the armies joined. They were weakened after Flaithbertach's madness, and outnumbered two to one since Flan Sinna had arrived. He crouched to one knee and stabbed his sword into the ground and wiping his hand in the dewy grass, he stared across the field at the men before him.

Through his remaining eye, he could see the red-and-blue banner of his father's men flapping in the wind some two hundred yards ahead. It was held high by a flag bearer among the other banners from those who had joined them, but he could not spy his father. His vision was not keen over distance, since he had started to rely on one eye. Looking for detail over distance caused his head to hurt.

He scanned the faces around him, then stood. He grabbed his sword from the grip of the earth and began to beat it on the metal boss of his shield, the clang of metal on metal joined the orchestra of sound around him. If you can imagine the sound of rage, then that is what you would hear as the two armies faced each other across the field, ready to charge and hack each other down at close quarters.

A hush fell over the gathered crowd as priests from both sides stepped forward to give their blessings. Though there were Norse and Frankish mercenaries scattered throughout, both armies were predominantly Christian, a battle fought between Christian Kings.

Black crows circled overhead in slow deliberate arcs, sensing that blood would be spilled. They called to each other lazily, they were relaxed for there would be plenty for them to gorge on this day. Priests dressed in black stood in front of the armed men and prayers were offered to God, the Father, and Jesus, the Savior, to bring victory to the righteous ones.

Ceallach gritted his teeth, eager for prayers to end and battle to begin. He held his sword tight in his right hand, his knuckles white as he knelt in prayer. "Dearest Lord Jesus," he offered quietly. "Guide my remaining eye to rest upon my father so I may find him. Guide my blade so I may cut him down and send him to hell where he belongs. Guide me, Lord Jesus." He felt a tear trickle down his face and watched it fall to the grass below. The priests retreated, their somber faces and tight lips showed little confidence, despite their prayers.

Horsemen rode forward as their riders drew their swords, the morning sun shone off the gleaming metal as the haze lifted and men stood up from their knees and began to clamor on their shields, as both sides of the battlefield rose to a deafening crescendo of bloodthirsty rage. Diarmuid, son of Ceirbeall, strong and straight, his jaw set and eyes determined, rode with great fury atop a black stallion, up and down the ranks of his father's army, carrying the banner high. He cried challenges for single combat, but no one moved. Ceallach fought the urge to step forward, he desperately wanted to take his brother's head from his shoulders, but it was his father he was here for.

The crows continued their lazy dance overhead, casting shadows below, and drums began to beat to a slow steady rhythm, as the tension mounted and the sky clouded over. Then, announced by the long low sound of a horn, there was movement. Who knows where it started, but many men were eager to spill blood and die in glory, others were eager to have it over and done with. Horses bolted as their riders tried to keep the terrified animals under control and men on foot charged like wild animals, axes, swords, and spears at the ready, to make short work of each other.

It was a scene to behold from above, the movement and color converged to become one, a marvel for the crows who waited to feast. The earth rumbled and shook, and the grass was trampled to dirt in a stampede of madness, as death came to the field below.

The two hundred yards between the two armies closed quickly and men died the instant both front lines collided, crashing into each other with a fury known only in hand-to-hand combat between armies. In the space of a moment, as both sides converged and collided to a sudden stop of crunching bone and shattered skulls, the initial injuries were sustained by impact rather than laceration. This was followed by the hacking and slashing of sharpened swords and axes as the blood began to follow and the ground ran red.

Ceallach had been overtaken by the first line or two of men, he heard the great crash as the lines of battle were joined. He roared and held his shield sturdy in front of him, as he smashed through to the other side where he could turn and slash at men on either side of him to cut a way through to his father. His sword gave him an advantage at close quarters over the spearmen who could not afford swords.

The ground already was slippery as it ran crimson. Ceallach had to take care to watch his right side to make up for his missing eye. He had experimented with keeping his shield on his right arm, but his left was no good to swing a sword. When he broke through the lines, he found himself surrounded by the enemy and immediately turned to his blind spot on the right to find a giant bearded man distracted by his comrades. He sunk his blade deep into the big man's side, bringing him down, then wrenched the blade free, as the big man died on the ground before him, creating some space.

There was no time to catch his breath, no time to pause. He turned to check his back, only to see more of his Munster cohorts driving their way forward with him. Almost every footman on both sides had now broken through the enemy lines and were in the thick of the fighting. The crows view from above saw a writhing shape below bulging and contracting, like a serpent about to vomit.

The Munstermen, although outnumbered two to one, were holding their own, Ceallach was driving forward, having dispatched several of the enemy without sustaining injury, though he was tiring. He sweated heavily and his head began to ache again. What if he collapsed in a fit of shaking? He would be cut down or wake up on a field of corpses.

He pressed forward, aiming to get to the back of the enemy lines where he might spy his father more easily.

Blood-soaked carnage surrounded him. It was difficult to tell if either army were getting the upper hand at this point. The screams of pain and fury were deafening, as all around, men on both sides fell, dead or injured. Ceallach joined the chorus of furious screams as he made eye contact with a Frankish mercenary. He was the enemy as far as Ceallach knew, the only hired swords on their side were Flaithbertach's Vikings.

Men dropped and warriors became corpses. The pace shifted as the fighting spread. This gave warriors on both sides a chance to take stock and see who they were fighting rather than blindly swinging and hacking.

Ceallach and the Frank looked one another in the eye, each man paused for a breath. Ceallach circled to his right, the other men around him were busy with their own problems. His head pounded now, he risked a quick glance to his right to check his blind spot. Seeing he was in the clear, he turned his attention back to the other warrior, who had spotted the distraction and slashed for Ceallach's unguarded shin.

Ceallach spotted the movement and dropped to his knees, bringing his shield up, he deflected the blow and jabbed forward and up with his own blade.

His eye pained him. He could feel the puss running down his face, the wound must have reopened. He could smell it too and felt like retching. He swallowed the impulse and ignored the pain in his head as he swung his sword in his right hand, pushing back to his feet, he moved toward his foe. He swung hard and fast in crossing slashes and butted the other man's shield, knocking him off balance.

He prepared to lift his sword for a killer blow, but his sword was as heavy as an anvil. He dropped it, fell to his knees and vomited the rabbit stew he had eaten for breakfast onto the ground before him, his chin was a stinking mess of blood, puss, and vomit. He couldn't move. He couldn't bear the weight of his shield in his left hand, so he let it fall by his side.

The Frankish mercenary stared in disbelief for a moment, but regained his senses as Ceallach fell forward to his hands and knees and vomited again. "I'll teach you some manners," he shouted in broken Gaelic, as he raised his sword to finish off this pitiful figure, only to be caught in the back of the head by an axe. He fell flat on his face in front of the vomiting wretch.

"Father," cried Ceallach. "Father, where are you?" His body was weak and his vision began to blur. He rolled to a seated position on his rump and wept. "Father, where are you?" he sobbed. He sat there weeping, the carnage surrounded him. What had the sell-sword shouted before he fell? "Teach me manners," he said. "You will teach me manners." Men fell around him, "Yes, Matudan, my father taught me manners, like you said, Matudan." Why hadn't he seen it before now? He sat and wailed as men screamed in agony about him. "Father…"

Whether he called for his blood father for vengeance or for his foster father for comfort, no one would know. Regardless, his cries of despair and grief were heard by the men about him. Despair from the son of a King is a dangerous thing. But the son of two Kings? It took hold in the minds of the men who saw him and spread quicker than any fever.

Ceallach sat and wept, and cried that all was lost and the men from Munster, who were close enough to hear and recognize Ceallach, saw that he had lost heart. Some fled, some were cut down as despair took their own hearts. Others fought on, but their weapons grew heavier and their arms grew sluggish as they watched their comrades turn and run or be cut down as their faces darkened with fear.

****

Finnan lay on his back, a dead man across his chest. Another dead man lay beside him, staring wide-eyed. A mounted soldier on top a black stallion thundered past, lashing down at the men below him with a heavy battle-axe.

He had to get up. He was not injured, at least, so far as he could tell. He pushed the corpse off and threw it to one side. He had lost his shield and weapon, but grabbed the axe from his recently departed bedfellow and got to his feet, quickly assessing the situation.

He wiped his muddied face to clear his vision, standing like a tightened bowstring, axe in hand, and ready to pounce.

It was not his preferred weapon, but he could handle a shorter battle-axe reasonably well. He took a moment to take stock of his position. He had been separated from his group in the first few moments of the battle.

The Munstermen around him were engaged with Norsemen. Why were there Norsemen fighting against Cormac? As far as he knew, the only Norsemen on this field were Flaithbertach's mercenaries. He had a bad feeling about this, but had no time to think on it as he ducked and rolled to narrowly avoid the heavy battle axe of the mounted rider who had come back around. The rider carried on past and did not turn back for another attempt at Finnan.

He regained his footing and moved toward the closest melee. He floored a Norse warrior with a blow to the back of the leg above the knee, opening a wide gash in his thigh muscle. This man would not walk again, but no matter, Finnan finished him with a blow to the head.

He moved on past a screaming man on his hands and knees, to confront another tall, skinny Norseman who came at him with no shield but a sword in each hand, hacking at him in turn with both weapons. Finnan had no defense but to back off, as he was without a shield and could not block two swords with an axe. As he moved to avoid the attacker, he heard a man screaming for his father and saw Munstermen cut down as they fled in fear. *Why do they flee,* he thought, as the Norseman swinging at him stumbled. He took his chance, quick from years of battle and training, he raised his arm and let his axe fly, catching his Norse attacker in the chest.

Finnan turned quickly to assess the situation and he saw that most of the Norsemen around him were busy cutting down the Munstermen. The man on his hands and knees, he realized, was his friend, Ceallach, weeping for his father and crying like a coward that there was no hope.

He had no time to think. He could see the fear and despair spreading through the Munstermen like a deadly red mist enveloping them. He grabbed the nearest weapon, a small Norse battle axe from the muddied ground under him and ran to his friend. "Ceallach," he screamed, as he swung the axe, catching his friend at the base of his jaw and opening his throat. "Ceallach," he cried again, cradling his friend in his arms, as the life drained from his body. He did not know why he called his name, the act was done.

****

Men screamed and horses whickered. There were flames, smoke, and the smell of blood in the air. The violence and cruelty stung MacGaman's eyes. He lived for it. He carried a long wooden staff of golden ash, holding it in both hands, an unconventional weapon for battle. Old fashioned and unpractical, but MacGaman was not a practical person.

"Finnan," he called. He could have taken him. The young warrior had not seen him. "Finnan," he said again, "fight me. Now is the time. Kill or be killed," he said.

Finnan turned and saw his old teacher standing tall, silhouetted in the smoke with still, silent warriors laying in the mud all around him. He felt the scars. He felt the pain. He felt the broken fingers, the bruised ribs, and the smashed teeth dealt out by this man emerging from the smoke in front of him, the smell of death was rife in the air.

"Finnan, fight me."

"MacGaman," Finnan said. "The pieces are in place."

"Aye," replied the old teacher. "Mine or yours?"

Finnan's shoulder was bleeding, he threw down his shield and swung the short sword he had taken from Ceallach at the older warrior, as a man on horseback sped past, hanging out of his saddle, a spear driven through his stomach. The man fell. The two men ignored him as they continued their fight which had lasted years. MacGaman deflected and parried, landing his own blow to Finnan's knee, knocking him off balance. Finnan did not fall, but caught the next blow, deflecting it over his head, rolling forward.

He turned, the old man was slowing down, sweat dripped from his brow and he breathed heavily. "MacGaman," Finnan said, "you were a cruel teacher."

"I was," replied the older man.

"I don't need to kill you. Your lessons kept me alive," Finnan said, out of breath.

They stared at each other, standing in the blood-soaked grass, the sounds of death and cruelty surrounded them, dimmed somewhat by the fires of the dying battle. "They have your Queen, Finnan."

Finnan stared at him dumbly. "They took her," MacGaman said again. "The black monk took her before his little play with the horse. He took her."

"You're a liar," Finnan said. "This is one of your chess moves. Why would he do that?"

The other man threw down his staff. "To trick Flan into fighting for Ceirbeall. It worked. He is too blind with madness to see through it. I can get you out of here," he said. "You'll not get her now. You can't kill them. Not now. I'll get you out of here, lad."

****

He is running under a clear blue sky, the damp grass is tickling his feet, he is late for his class. It is warm and he is sweating. He feels his heart pounding in his chest, as his legs carry him past the chapel toward the abbot's hut where they will meet. A sudden stab of pain shoots up his leg, forcing him to skip a step and hop. He stops short. It's gone. He pauses a second, seeing the monks in the distant fields bent over their crops as if in worship. The silence is broken by the chattering of birds as they call to each other. Was there something he had to do? he thinks to himself, *What was it? What did I forget?*

"The horse," he said aloud, remembering he had to move the horse. "I don't have a horse," he whispered to himself. There were no horses at the monastery.

He dismisses the thought and recites as he walks. Greek, as they had been taught. He practices his numbers.

"Alpha..." He hears the call of a crow. It is watching him, standing directly in his path, its ebony eyes stare him down.

"Beta..." his voice is hoarse.

"Gamma..." says the crow. What is this nonsense?

"Delta..." The horse...the pain in his legs is back. The horse is dead. The crow. The crow stares at him, "What do you want? Get away. Get off me. Let me up."

He can't move. The horse is dead. The pain in his legs. Warmth.

The crow reaches forward and extends his neck. Opening his mouth, he releases a hoarse cry from where he stands on the flank of the bleeding horse. "Your lessons," croaks the crow, and flies away.

"Alpha…" He is late now, he must stop daydreaming and get to his lessons. He smells smoke. It was too late for breakfast and too early for the evening meal. The monks fast in between.

"Beta…" He sees the abbot with the other students. "Cormac…" he is greeted. "Cormac, have you left us, Cormac. Cormac?"

"I'm here, abbot. I'm here. Alpha, Beta, Gamma, Delta. I'm ready for the lessons, abbot." It was wet. His face was wet, but when he looked up at the sky, it was clear.

The crow again. "Cormac," it screeched. He looked down at the crow. It stared back at him through gleaming black eyes.

"Cormac, it's over," the crow said, speaking in a harsh, shrill voice. "Look what's become of you," It's all spinning. He sees the horse. He's on the ground in the wet grass. It's dark. The rain. Burning. The warm flicker of firelight to his right is comforting…but wrong, somehow. His legs are trapped. It's his horse. His horse is dead. He can't move. His men. Where are his men?

"They're all dead."

"Where are my men?"

"Dead… Dead…dead…dead…dead."

"Flaithbertach…it's you. Thank God. We need to leave, Flaithbertach. Help me with this horse."

"I didn't fall, Cormac. I jumped. You still don't see. You are still blind…I jumped."

"You jumped," Cormac said.

"I jumped. I jumped because I knew they would leave you." Realization dawned on Cormac's face as he came to his senses. He was not badly injured. Between the two of them, they could move the horse and regroup…and…maybe…

"You jumped from the horse. That's why they deserted me. You played me false. It was all a farce," Cormac said. "Beware the serpent who falls."

Flaithbertach hunkered down beside his incapacitated King, and rubbed his knife up and down his thigh.

"I'm here for you now. That's all you need to know."

Cormac's heart sank as for the first time, he saw Flaithbertach for what he really was. The devil. His friend, his ally, his brother of the cloth. He had been betrayed. Flaithbertach had insisted they fight this hopeless battle.

"Why?" he said. Did he really care about the reasons at this stage? He knew it was over.

"I'm taking the crown, Cormac. The crown and your head. A great bishop makes a poor King, and you, my friend, are both. A bishop St. Peter would be proud of, but a King who can't fit the crown. I'd make a terrible bishop, in fact,

I'm a terrible monk. I've spilled more blood than I can tell. That's what makes Kings."

He raised his knife and examined the blade. "Killing men makes Kings," he said, and brought the tip of the blade to Cormac's throat, drawing a trickle of blood.

"No," said Cormac. He was not afraid to die, but what terrified him was the prospect of the mad monk taking his kingdom. There was only hatred and malice left in Flaithbertach. He could see that now.

"Yes," said Flaithbertach.

"Killing men makes Kings, but killing Kings makes great Kings."

The tip of the knife pierced his skin and dug into his throat. He felt the warm gush of blood spread through his neck as the pain set his mind on fire. The blade dug deeply, his arms beat wildly. He could taste the blood in his mouth as he choked on it.

The crow came back. "Alpha," it screeched.

"Beta," Cormac continued. "Gamma..." he recited, smiling, as he picked up his pace to a run. He was late for his lesson.

Chapter Fourteen

The battle ended with the remnants of the defeated Munster army being chased into the forest and run down. It became clear that the Munstermen could not hope to win. They were sorely outnumbered. Those who fled first made it far enough away to avoid being hunted down and killed, like dogs for the crows to feed on.

The others who fought and remained were massacred. Slowly, the ebb of the battle leaned to one side and slowly but surely, Munstermen dropped and died. Ironic, that it was honor that doomed these men who had stood by their King and fought bravely for their kingdom. Cormac's speech had inspired them to die with him. They stayed and fought and there came a point when it was impossible to leave. It was impossible to escape the massacre.

Finnan found himself in the trees to the east. His Queen was lost to him in the carnage. MacGaman, his old teacher, had taken him under the pretense of a prisoner and brought him as far as he could in safety. "Wait until the pieces are in place," he had told him before leaving.

His only hope now was to find his King or some of his men. The forest was dark, mist rose from the ground. *Which way was west,* he thought? The battle was west. Which way had Cormac ridden? He did not know. He was lost and he had no weapon.

Suddenly, there was a sound behind him as a man ran from the bushes, his eyes were wild and his bearded face was splattered with blood. He charged straight for Finnan. A Munsterman, Finnan guessed from the fact that he was fleeing. "Where is everybody?" Finnan shouted. "Where is the King?"

"The King is dead," the man shouted, shaking with fear. He got up and ran again.

Finnan pounced on him and pinned him to the ground. "Where is the King?" he asked again.

"Dead. Dead," the man replied, staring back up at Finnan through wild, maddened eyes. "He is dead. He cut off his head. The dark man cut off his head." He fell onto his back and gazed at the canopy above, his eyes wide then laughed loud and long, his body was cold and he trembled.

Finnan heard movement in the bush and the soft murmur of voices. "Quiet," he hissed, but the man continued to laugh. Finnan placed his hand over the man's mouth to keep him quiet.

The King is dead, Finnan thought. Could it be true? They were heavily outnumbered. It must have been a massacre.

The voices grew louder, several men were approaching. The man tried to cry out. "Quiet," Finnan whispered. "They're not our people. Be quiet."

The man continued to resist and bit Finnan's hand. Finnan reached for a knife in the man's belt and pushed it up through the soft flesh under his chin, into his brain. His eyes widened for a second, then relaxed and closed.

Finnan closed his eyes and slowed his breath, trying to relax. He had killed two men from his own army today. He lay in silence and waited for the voices to move on. Four men, he could see through the undergrowth. One of them, a larger man, was carrying a small bundle of rags.

"Who was that dark man?" one asked. "It doesn't matter, we just need to get the hell out of here," the voices trailed off. Dark man, Finnan had heard. He needed to get away from here and his best bet was to head in the opposite direction. Hopefully with some luck, he could link up with some survivors. If there were any left that was.

He could not see the sun in the dark forest and the moss grew all around the trees, so he could not tell which direction he was headed. He was truly lost.

He gathered dry moss from some of the nooks and crannies under the trees and walked throughout the day. He did not risk a fire the first night, but found what shelter he could under an old oak tree. It was cold and wet, it rained through the night and soaked his clothes to the skin. The wound on his shoulder felt like it would bring on a fever, it was hot; his head pained him.

The second day, he walked all day without meeting a soul or hearing anything. He guessed he had traveled some miles from the battleground now and hoped he was traveling in the southwest for Munster. He did not care if he was caught at this stage. He didn't even know if he would return to Munster. What would he do there? Watch it be torn apart or conquered by its neighbors?

He sat on a fallen tree on the edge of a clearing and after collecting himself, set to gathering some firewood. He would risk a fire tonight or risk dying of the cold or fever. He had managed to collect enough dry moss to catch a spark from his flint and soon had a fire blazing.

****

The flames of his campfire danced high into the air and brought comfort to his weary, battle-worn bones. His shoulder ached. He placed his knife on the stones at the edge of the fire, the blade within the flames, and watched it as it turned red. Time passed unknown to him and darkness fell.

He removed his cloak and took off his leather armor to expose his damaged shoulder. Blood and white puss oozed from the gaping wound. The skin was hot to touch.

He turned the knife around in his hand, its heat reflected off his face. He pressed it hard against the open cut in his shoulder and heard a hiss as his skin burned and he could smell the cooking flesh. At least it would close the wound and maybe, with luck, he would recover. He held it tight against his skin for as long as he could bear the pain, until he dropped back onto the ground, unconscious.

He fell into a dreamless sleep, the pain still gnawed at his shoulder and woke to the sound of a voice. "Hello. Hello, friend. Are you well?" it said. "Hello, friend?"

Finnan sat up. It was still nighttime, still dark, and the fire was still burning.

"I took the liberty of keeping your fire going," the voice said. An old man sat by Finnan's fire. "You were out cold, you would have frozen to death out here, my friend. What brings you out here anyway?" the man pressed. "You are a traveler?"

His new companion had kind eyes and smiled. "Who are you?" Finnan asked.

"A traveler," replied the stranger. "Just a traveler. I will leave you alone if you want, but you do not look so good and I have enough food to share. Goat's cheese, bread..." he laughed as Finnan's face changed when he mentioned food and tossed him a loaf of bread and a leather pouch of ale.

"Eat and drink deep, my friend, you look like you need it."

Finnan tore a lump of bread and gulped the ale down, he had not realized it was two days since he last ate. He was ravenous and didn't care if this was a trick. He would be glad to die on a full stomach.

"You would be glad to die on a full stomach," laughed the visitor.

Finnan stopped chewing and looked up. "Who are you?" he said again.

His visitor was an old man. Clean-shaven, white-haired, with a pious look about him. He did not sound like a foreigner, but his slightly accented words suggested he had traveled from this island and spoke other tongues.

"Does it matter?" asked the man. "Is it not enough that we are here now, breaking bread as friends?"

"You have word of the battle?" Finnan asked.

"The men of Munster were defeated. Their King is dead," replied the man. He smiled sadly, "This news troubles you, I can see. Where will you go?"

Many priests, merchants, whores, and sell-swords would have traveled with or close by the moving troops, administering their services either good or bad, where they could be offered. Finnan surmised this man was one such merchant or maybe a priest.

"Honestly," he said, beginning to feel better, "I thought I would die here tonight until I lit that fire and the warmth put some life into me. France maybe. York. I don't know. Everybody wants a good sword. Maybe I'll just disappear. Wouldn't that be nice if I could just disappear?"

"Wouldn't it be nice?" echoed the stranger. "It would indeed. Sell your sword. Why not go to a monastery? Why not forsake the sword for the cross?" he smiled but the question was not in jest.

"Me, a monk?" he laughed. "The other soldiers used to think I wanted men because I wouldn't fuck whores when they were about…but the truth is," he paused. Why was he telling this old man his secrets? What harm did it do now, he supposed.

"Go on," the stranger encouraged softly. "Tell me."

"The truth is, the woman I loved and served all my life is gone to God knows where. I could never have her anyway," he laughed and fell back on the grass, looking up at the stars as the sky began to clear. "She could never be mine because she was my Queen, and I, her servant, and I served her and her husband faithfully until the end."

The old man did not reply. Finnan sat in silence for a moment, lying on his back, looking up at the sky before continuing, "My King is dead, my Queen is gone. Yes, I think I'll just be a sell-sword and kill men in a foreign land for a few years." He laughed but his eyes were downcast.

These were his choices. Kill men, or become a man of the cloth. One as bad as the other.

"If you travel east, as the crow flies, for two days, you will find your Queen. Beware the mad monk, the man in black."

Finnan blinked. Did he hear that correctly?

"What?" Finnan asked. "What did you just say?"

Silence.

He sat up. The fire which had been burning brightly was low, embers in the ground. The camp was empty, save for him. No bag of food, no bladder of ale, and no visitor. The food was real, he felt better for having eaten it. He could taste the remnants of the bread and the goat's cheese. *Travel east for two days,* he thought. The man in black, the mad monk. Flaithbertach. Flaithbertach was the man in black. That is who he overhead the soldiers after the battle, speaking of. Beware the man in black?

What was this? He knew Flaithbertach was dangerous. Always suspected it and never trusted him.

He threw some more sticks on the embers and lay down to get some sleep. In the morning, he would head east for two days and see what he would see.

Chapter Fifteen

Flaithbertach was stripped of his armor and his abbot's robes, and sold into slavery to the very men he had hired to protect him. He was a prisoner of Torgny. The Norseman pushed him into Ceirbeall's bride's tent and flung him to the ground before his former Queen.

The groveling Flaithbertach was to be a gift to the new Queen of Leinster. He was thrown to the ground before the recently widowed and newlywed Queen. He landed in a heap at the foot of her bed, on the dusty ground of her tent.

"Beg, priest," Torgny told him.

"Please, my Queen," cried Flaithbertach. "I did not want him to die. He was like a brother to me." He sobbed and wept in the dirt, snot dripped from his nose and mixed with the dry dusty soil below, as he pushed back up to his elbows.

The Norseman kicked him hard into the ribs, sending him forward onto his belly again, to prostrate before the Queen. She recoiled, her eyes were wide, and she trembled with rage.

"What are you doing here," she cried. "Why have you brought him here. Get this demon out of my sight. Get out of here," she screamed at them. She grabbed a wooden plate by her bedside and threw it. It missed them and flew outside the tent.

At this, Flaithbertach rose again, his chained hands held out in front, imploring. The Norseman stepped forward and grabbed Flaithbertach by the hair. He pulled him from the tent.

Ceirbeall smiled to himself as he watched Torgny drag Flaithbertach toward his group to depart. His wedding gift to his wife was to convince her that Flaithbertach had been justly punished by being sold into a life of slavery to his former guards.

How cheaply they were bought. How easily they turned. Maybe this would convince her tight legs to spread for him tonight. She had been offered by Flan to seal Ceirbeall's claim over Munster, having spent only hours as a widow.

Ceirbeall had her watched in case she tried to take her life to join her former husband. "I want no ropes or blades near that bitch," he had shouted at his men. *Willing or not, I'll be in there*, he thought.

Their alliance had been worthwhile when it lasted, but now, someone had to take the blame for the death of the King of Thomand, and it might as well be the one who was responsible. The Norse leader unchained Flaithbertach and patted him on the cheek with his palm, as a beautiful white horse was led forward. He took the reins of the magnificent animal as Flaithbertach stood with his eyes downcast, shoulders hunched, and wept like a child.

How the mighty have fallen, Ceirbeall thought.

Torgny then took a thick fur cloak from the rump of the horse, draped it over Flaithbertach and handed him the reins to the noble beast. Flaithbertach straightened and mounted the animal. The Vikings before him parted to make way. Flaithbertach looked toward Ceirbeall and raised the stump of a forefinger in salute. He smiled and turned to ride away, as the Vikings fell in behind him.

Ceirbeall's jaw fell open as he watched the mad monk depart at the head of a small Norse army.

****

Gormfhlaith sat in her tent, tense and shaken. Why had he come to her? The mad monk was afraid of nothing she knew, he would rather burn in hell for eternity than beg and cry before a woman.

She was thinking about this when her husband came to her. The sun had gone down since Flaithbertach's departure, and a brazier burned in the middle of the tent.

"Did you like my gift, my Queen?" asked Ceirbeall.

She stiffened at his voice.

They buried her husband during the ceremony at first light and she was a married woman and a Queen again by mid-morning. Married to the man who may have cut her husband's head from his shoulders. It was either Ceirbeall or Flaithbertach. Flaithbertach had got the blame, but she wasn't so sure. The Abbot of Innis Caithigh was too clever by far, to get caught out like this.

"Your gift," she said through clenched teeth. She felt like leaping at him and ripping his ears from the side of his head with her teeth.

"Yes, my Queen. My gift. Come now. The monk has been sold into slavery."

Gormfhlaith noticed his voice was unsteady. He grabbed a goblet and poured himself wine and swayed slightly as he undressed. *He's drunk,* Gormfhlaith thought.

He left his weapons outside. He was taking no chances with her, "Take off your clothes, my Queen. It is time we consummated our marriage and you bore some children from someone who can actually achieve it."

She obeyed and removed her clothes in front of her new husband. She concentrated hard to take her mind away from this place as she prepared herself to take him inside her.

She lay back and spread her legs for him. She could smell the wine on his breath as he lay on top of her.

"Your gift," she said, as he slipped inside her.

Ceirbeall smiled and grunted like an animal, as she turned him over on his back, moving up and down on him as her arms squeezed through the bed sheets. "Your gift," she said again, arching back up as Ceirbeall's hands moved all over her. She quickened her pace, her body excited not for the physical feelings of being joined in bed with her new King, but by the excitement of what was about to happen. The excitement of the gift. The real gift, Flaithbertach's gift.

She smacked her hands hard down on Ceirbeall's chest, planting the knife which Flaithbertach had left as he lay on his belly before her, snorting in the ground. She jumped off him as blood began to surge from a gaping hole just below his chest. She still had time. There was life in him for a few moments. She still had time to make him suffer, she thought, as she pulled out the blade and stabbed frantically at his abdomen.

Ceirbeall stared at his naked blood-soaked wife and opened his mouth, but could find no voice as he bled to death, lying on the bed where he had tried to consummate his marriage. He died in silence, seeing finally that the mad monk had gotten the better of him.

****

Finnan woke in the dark, the sun had yet to rise. The driving rain poured through the canopy of the forest into his makeshift shelter. The morning was full of dreams of warmth and comfort, with a belly full of food. Sizzling pork and steaming warm bread, hot from the oven, but his body could ignore his wet arse no longer and he woke.

He would ride to Flan Sinna's camp this morning and there, he would find death, for his chances of success were slim. There would be no flight to France or Ulster. Shivering in the predawn dark, he thought about this. He was not afraid to die for his King and Queen, he just wished it didn't have to be on a hungry stomach on a shitty damp morning like this.

The sun came up and brought light to a dull August day, rays of sun tried desperately to break through an angry blanket of gray clouds. Finnan covered the remains of his fire, long since extinguished in the driving rain, and tore down his shelter. He set out, cold, damp, and hungry.

After trudging through the undergrowth on a small game trail for four hours, he smelled food. *Porridge maybe,* he thought. He ignored his stomach growling and set forward to see smoke rising from a camp and a group of six on a hunting excursion, judging from the elk meat hanging from the trees. It had stopped raining and the morning sun made its way through the trees. He circled around the camp, a damp fog in the air combined with the skinny beech trees masked his presence.

Their accents suggested they were Leinstermen, but he wasn't sure until he made the blue and white colors of Ceirbeall on the shield strung across the back of one man taking a piss, the steam rising through the morning air.

Finnan had no weapons, having lost the knife. He had no problem killing a man with his bare hands, but to do that quietly was a bigger challenge. He threw a small stone at the pissing man to get his attention and grabbed a fist-sized rock. When the man turned, he let a short whistle. The man finished his business and headed in Finnan's direction. Who knows why he thought it was a good idea to walk toward the sound of a man whistling, but the victory had left them complacent and arrogant. Besides, Finnan was out of options at this stage.

When the man drew close, Finnan rose to his feet, lunged forward, and head-butted the man in the face, he heard the nose crack and could feel the man's teeth crunching against his scalp. The man fell back, his open mouth reeked of beer and blood. Finnan pounced on him and smashed his skull in a dull wet crunch with the rock.

Finnan hurriedly threw the man's woolen cloak over him and pulled up the hood, keeping the man's sword and shield in hand, he headed back for the camp. It would not be long before they found the corpse and these hunters were undoubtedly skilled trackers, Finnan thought. They would find him before long. He had only one option, which was a long shot. Hopefully, the scent of ale off the man he had just killed was a sign that these men were groggy from drinking and overconfident from victory.

He wandered lazily to the edge of the camp. "You took your time. Pissing like a fucking bear," one of them said to him.

He said nothing and kept his head down. This man was tending to the horses. He would tackle him last. The other four were sitting around the fire, eating gray gruel which resembled a shit gone bad. It had been dished out from a pot hanging over the campfire.

Finnan grabbed a bowl and leaned close to the fire between two of the men, his hood covered his face. Nobody paid any attention. He grabbed the pot and swung it hard to his left, catching one of the men in the face. The man fell back, and Finnan threw the steaming hot gruel in the face of the other man, as he raised his head to see what the commotion was. By now, the other two men at the fireside were on their feet, but not quick enough, as Finnan smashed one of them in the face with the steel rim of his shield, killing him instantly, as he kicked the burning logs toward the other man, before jumping over them to slash hard at his left knee, cutting through to the bone, he took the man down.

He turned immediately to take care of the two men he had incapacitated and struck gruel-face in the side of the head with his shield. He swung his sword at the man he had struck with the pot and caught him with a lucky strike to the jugular, blood sprayed onto Finnan's face. A sloppy strike, but effective.

The one whose knee he had cut to the bone lay on the ground, screaming like a trapped animal, he was no threat and could do little else but cradle his knee as the blood poured from it. He would not last long.

Two left. He wanted to take one alive. The man he had struck with his shield was stunned. Finnan knocked him out cold with a blow to the temple. He would do for a hostage.

The last man was advancing on Finnan with a sword, a sly smile across his scarred face. He didn't seem too bothered about his fallen comrades. He had probably seen enough death in the last two days to care about it.

"Little man," he sneered. "Little man wants to kill him some Leinstermen?"

"Little man has just killed himself four Leinstermen, you half-witted shit, and you're next," Finnan replied, as he lunged his sword. His opponent had strong forearms and handled a sword well, but his movements were slow and his breath smelled of ale. Finnans arms were weak and his shoulder ached as he swung his sword.

The clash of metal rang out through the morning air, the injured man had stopped screaming.

Finnan could tell this was the sort of man who beat the camp whores and raped innocents for the fun of it during a plunder. He dropped the shield to fight his opponent with a sword only.

His opponent smiled when he saw this, he dropped his shield as well. He circled around the Munsterman as the mist rose from the forest floor, as if to shroud the men. "Finding it tough are you, little man?" he asked, grinning as Finnan dropped to his knees. Finnan hated men like this. Men who fought and killed for pleasure rather than a cause. The man stepped closer, getting ready to make the kill.

"Put the pieces in place," he heard MacGaman say. One of the most skilled soldiers in the army of Munster does not drop to his knees, to be butchered by a sheep-shagging murderer like this, he thought. He ducked and rolled to one side as the man dropped his guard, and rose to wrap his good arm around his opponent's sword arm, he wrenched it hard and fast and heard it snap. Blood stained the man's sleeve where the bone had come through the skin.

The man screamed in agony and dropped his sword, as Finnan twisted further and pressed his sword to the back of the man's neck. His enemy's eyes widened as he pushed the blade through. He pulled his blade free and let the lifeless corpse drop to the ground and went to check on the one he left alive. The morning light revealed a face familiar to him.

****

People were buzzing to and fro about the camp, preparing to tear down the tents and march their separate ways. As far as most were concerned, there was peace between Ceirbeall and Flan.

Soldiers went back and forth, tending to their animals, preparing them for the march. Foot soldiers readied their weapons and prepared to move out.

Flags flapped in the late summer breeze. The incessant rain which had turned the battlefield of two days previous into a fly-infested swamp of corpses had subsided.

Flan Sinna slept the sleep of Kings. His son-in-law was dead, but peace prevailed. Flaithbertach had been sold into slavery to the Vikings in punishment for kidnapping his daughter and she was returned safe and sound. A widow no more, she was a Queen again, having been the Queen of two Kingdoms in the space of a week.

And so, Flan Sinna slept a dreamless sleep, until it was shattered by the screams of a woman as the Leinstermen seized his daughter who had fled her tent covered in blood. It was not long before they discovered the corpse and guessed what happened.

Flan threw the sheepskin covers off him and jumped from his bed, knocking the clay jug of wine to the floor in the process. He staggered out of the gloomy tent, still drowsy, the sunlight hurt his eyes. It took him a moment to come to his senses and remember where he was.

A crowd had gathered at Ceirbeall's tent, men from both sides, frantic and angry, with weapons drawn. He sensed the tension as he approached, he heard raised voices and the mention of his daughter's name.

The crowd grew as he approached. "Out of my way," he roared. "I'm the bloody King, get the hell out of my way. What is all this? Put down your weapons," he shouted, as he pushed his way through the fools in front of him. He did not notice the hush descend when he arrived and how those around him would not meet his gaze.

He stopped dead in his tracks, and stared, stunned. His daughter was kneeling on the ground, bound by the wrists. She was naked, covered in blood. Diarmuid, son of Ceirbeall, stood before him, with a sword to her throat.

"What is this?" he shouted, and barged through the crowd, punching the first Leinsterman who approached him straight in the nose, breaking it.

Diarmuid grabbed Gormfhlaith's hair and pulled her head closer to him, sword to her throat, stopping Flan in his tracks. He could see now why his men were holding off.

The blur of sleep cleared from his mind all of a sudden and the anger gave way to the logic which made him a great King. He saw his daughter was not injured and realized that it was not her blood. Judging from the current state of affairs, it could belong to only one man. Ceirbeall was dead by his daughter's hand.

"Diarmuid," said Flan, his throat was dry. "Diarmuid, think. I know this is not how you wanted it to happen, but you are now King." He let these words ring in the air for a moment, as a crow cawed overhead, sensing more bloodshed to gorge himself on.

I am King, thought Diarmuid. *I am King.* Sweat rolled down his brow. He wanted nothing more than to jerk his arm swiftly and open the whore's throat in front of her father. *What then, though?* he thought, as he looked around. Every man here had a hand on his weapon. There could be no clear winner to the fight which would ensue.

"Diarmuid," Flan said again. "This is not how I wanted things either, but you are King. Let us keep our alliance."

"And what of vengeance?" Diarmuid shouted. "What of my right to vengeance?"

"I cannot give you vengeance," replied Flan. "But I can give you friendship. If you harm my daughter now, you and your men will die here today and it will be all for nothing."

Diarmuid tightened the grip on Gormfhlaith's hair and shouted, "She will be dead and I will have my vengeance, and we will see who else dies after that, old man."

"Maybe," said Flan, as he lowered his hands and walked forward. "Maybe. But if you fall, who will be King in your place? Leinster will mourn Ceirbeall, but they have a powerful King to take his place. If you fall, and if you kill my daughter, I will make sure you do fall," he said, "Who will take your place?"

Diarmuid saw sense in the old man's words, but did not release his grip on the sword at Gormfhlaith's neck.

"No one will," Flan answered for him. "No one will take your crown. Your cousins and your son will squabble over it and your brother will eventually raise an army from Munster and come and take a divided kingdom."

Diarmuid did not answer. The two men stared at one another. Flan did not want bloodshed. Not now. He could see the anger in Diarmuid's eyes. Diarmuid was ready to risk immediate death and all-out war on two fronts for this.

They did not notice the crowd part as a rider guided his horse through the angry crowd. Flan went on, "I will offer you my daughter's hand in marriage as a sign of good will and the continuing friendship and support of my Kingdom, if you will honor your father's original agreement."

Gormfhlaith had sat in silence. She had in the space of moments accepted the fact that this would be the extent of her vengeance and that she could now die and join her beloved Cormac. But at hearing her father's offer, she looked up, red in the face. "I will not," she screamed, and struggled to break free, the knife drew a trickle of blood to drip down her neck, mixing with the blood of her dead husband.

"I will not," she screamed again. "I am not your pawn. I am not your property. You will use me no more," she shouted and spat at her father, her struggles deepened the wound in her neck.

Diarmuid lowered his knife and released her. She fell forward to her hands and knees, as the rider approach.

"I accept," said Diarmuid, seeing how angry this made his hostage. He did not have to kill her to take his vengeance. He dropped his sword and approached Flan with a hand extended in friendship.

"You will not take her," the rider said. "Gormfhlaith, my Queen, get up. I will take you if you will come."

The rider, tall and strong, rode on a black stallion, holding the reins in his left hand, he held a tattered, red Munster flag on a makeshift pole high in his right hand. Piercing-blue eyes stared out through a face stained dark with blood.

Three human heads hung from a rope draped around the horse's neck. Their mouths were agape, their jaws twisted in anguish, as the flies fed on the exposed stumps of their necks.

"I am Finnan," the man said, "and I have come for the Queen."

Finnan tossed the severed heads on the ground in front of the men. They had died some days ago and were already beginning to stink. Flies buzzed around the pulp of the eyeballs. Diarmuid recognized them as his father's soldiers. Toughened fighters. For one man to take them down, he had to be a great warrior.

"Well, my friend, she's not going anywhere," Diarmuid replied, "Because you may have just heard – there's to be a wedding. My future father-in-law here beside you," he gestured to Flan Sinna who stood with his mouth agape at this new turn of events, "just offered me your Queen, so I don't really give a rat's shit who you are and I think my first act as King will be to cut your head off."

The stranger eyed Flan Sinna quietly and did not move.

"Take him," Diarmuid ordered his men. "Don't kill him. I want that pleasure."

"I have your son," the stranger said in a low voice.

He has my son? How does he have his son, he thought to himself, as the stranger took a small bundle wrapped in cloth from a worn leather pouch around his neck.

"My son?" asked Diarmuid, with twitch of his head. "You have my son. What do you mean you have my son? Flan, what does he mean? My son is on a hunting party with your men."

"Diarmuid," Flan stuttered, "I sent your men. Those men," he pointed at the rotting heads.

The stranger tossed the bundle on the ground, "Open it. He's still alive. The blood is still warm. I have no reason to kill him. Not yet."

Diarmuid bent to pick up the bundle of cloth, damp with blood. He uncovered a fore finger bearing the ring he had given his own son on his last birthday. The blood was indeed still warm. This could not have been cut more than an hour before.

Diarmuid's right eye twitched. He gripped the cloth and pulled it apart, letting the blood-severed digit fall to the ground.

"Meet me on the ridge before sundown and we'll make the exchange. You will provide me with two horses and a bow and quiver of arrows before I leave here. If I'm followed, your son dies. If you try to surround me on the hill, your son dies. Just you, Flan, and Gormfhlaith."

"Get him the horses—" Diarmuid said.

"But, my King," his men interjected.

"NOW," roared Diarmuid, turning on them. "Get him the horses and whatever the hell else he wants now. Flan, it seems we have an issue with this wedding we were planning."

The horses were brought within minutes as the stranger waited silently, unmoving atop his horse, the flies still buzzed about the heads.

"Have her cleaned up. She is a Queen," he said and turned and rode out of the camp.

****

The ridge was in the mountains. It overlooked all the land around and could only be approached from the east and west. Outside of the tree line, it had a view from all around. The stranger had chosen well. Flan and Diarmuid would approach from the east, riding an hour through the forest, then up through the rocky slopes, until the horses would have to be abandoned for the men and their captive to continue on foot. The exchange, one assumed, would be made at the top of the ridge, where both sides would part company, Diarmuid and Flan heading east, back the way they had come, Finnan and Gormfhlaith heading west, a short ride to the narrow wooden bridge which crossed the river carrying water to the villages below.

There was a chill in the air as summer gave way to autumn, Finnan's tattered Munster flag snapped in the wind on the makeshift pole he had salvaged. He had bound Feidhlim's hands behind his back and propped him atop one of the horses. A noose around his neck was tied to the lonely, gnarled tree which guarded the ridge like an old sentry. Everything was set as he watched the three figures approach.

Diarmuid was furious. The anger consumed him. He wanted to thrash this bitch who had murdered his father and put his son in harm's way. He stared at her as they scrambled up the rocks. His bride. He wanted to smash one of those rocks over her head. They climbed on up, almost in sight of the ridge. He could see some movement by the tree up above, still too far too make out clearly.

Once the exchange was made, it was three on two. Three on one. The woman didn't count. The wind was picking up and it would be dark soon.

"Far enough," he heard a voice call. "Send the Queen up alone,"

Diarmuid looked up. He had been lost in thought. He could see the figures on the top clearly now, silhouetted by the setting sun. His son was sitting atop one of the horses he had gifted the stranger, a noose around his neck tied to the old tree on top. He stopped as he was told. Not seeing another choice.

"Let her go," said Flan. "Once we have your son, we can make our way around. We'll catch up to them. They'll not be able to mount up until they cross the bridge."

"And it'll be three on one," Diarmuid said half to himself.

Three on two, Gormfhlaith thought. She would fight her proposed husband and father to the death before she would go back with them. She was so tired. It was time for this to end.

"Go," snarled Diarmuid, and without so much as a glance at either of them, she started the scramble up to the old tree, some fifty yards ahead.

Finnan's arrow was drawn and trained on the two men as Gormfhlaith approached. "Take the two horses to the bridge," he said to her. "If I'm not there before the sun goes down, then light the bridge and ride."

"They're going to come for you," she said.

"They may," he said, gesturing to the boy on the horse with the rope around his neck, "but this one's not going to be much help to them."

Flan watched his daughter disappear over the hill. He could not make out their conversation, but he assumed the stranger had been warned. He knew his daughter had no love for him after what had happened.

"Send the other back," Finnan shouted down. "You come up here, alone." With that, he lowered his arrow and drew a knife. He placed it to the back of Feidhlim's hamstring and pulled it hard across to cut him deep. Feidhlim, grunted through a gagged mouth and the horse whickered, smelling the blood, ready to bolt and let the man dangle. Finnan calmed the animal with a stroke to the head and some soothing words.

"He's all yours, but I've cut your son bad. You'll have to get him back and close the wound quickly before he bleeds out."

"Flan," shouted Diarmuid. "Tend to my son." With that, he scrambled as fast as he could around the side, on up the mound, hoping to cut Finnan off, or at least close the distance.

Finnan made his way down the slope, having expected something like this would happen. He could see Diarmuid circling around under him and knew Flan was on the way up. It didn't matter. Diarmuid was going to cut him off.

He stopped. The two men looked at each other. Diarmuid saw the stranger draw his bow and stopped when he realized what was about to happen. Flan was still minutes away and the useless old man was too slow for this rocky terrain anyway. The stranger aimed back up the hill at the horse bearing Diarmuid's son, who was bleeding heavily, and loosened the arrow, catching the animal directly in the back thigh.

146

Finnan did not even pause to see what would happen next. He jumped down the rock slopes and didn't bother to look behind. He knew Diarmuid would have men already making their way up the slopes in pursuit.

Diarmuid ignored Finnan and ran for his son who was hanging by the neck and bleeding to death. He drew his sword and slashed at the rope his boy dangled from. The boy fell in a heap on the ground, wheezing and coughing. By this time, Flan Sinna and the men he had waiting were in view.

"After them," he shouted. "They can't mount up until a mile after the bridge. After them. I'm going to fucking skin them. After them," he screamed and shook with rage. He had to get his son back to the camp. He was not conscious and his leg was a bloody mess. The boy was only seventeen. He was strong and would make it if they were quick. Then, out of the corner of his eye, he saw a flicker of light. *The bridge is burning,* he thought in dismay. "The bridge is burning," he shouted.

****

Gormfhlaith had reached the bridge and had to lead the two horses across one by one, as she stepped over the bundles of rushes and twigs tied along the base of it. Finnan had been busy, on the other side, she saw a torch and a flint and knew what she had to do. By the time she saw Finnan sprinting toward the bridge, the sun was gone and dusk had fallen. She already had the torch lit and ready to go.

"Fire it up," shouted Finnan. "Fire it up and let's get out of here," he shouted, as he crossed.

She saw some men come into view over the hill and set the torch to the twigs and then threw it out to the middle of the bridge. The wind which had been rising steadily took hold and by the time the men had reached the edge of the gorge, the bridge was an inferno, ready to collapse.

Her engagement to Diarmuid, son of Ceirbeall, had been short lived, just like her marriage to his father.

She joined her rescuer. There was little time for celebration as they led their horses down to the flatter terrain where they mounted up and rode west for the Kingdom of Munster, where they would surely find allies, unaware of the fact that Flaithbertach and his Norse mercenaries had a head start on them.

147

CPSIA information can be obtained
at www.ICGtesting.com
Printed in the USA
LVHW080707030620
656993LV00012B/593

9 781643 788425